The Return of a Cowboy

Crossroads Creek Cowboys

Elsie Davis

Sweet Romance Publishing

Sweet Romance Publishing

Sweetromancepublishing.com

PO Box 778

Liberty, NC 27298

1 John 5:14

"This is the confidence that we have in our relationship with God: If we ask for anything in agreement with his will, he listens to us."

Chapter One

♥

"TOBY, WE NEED TO leave like five minutes ago," Seth called out down the hallway, hoping to get his son motivated to move along. It was his first day in a new school, and therefore, important to make a good impression. Something Seth had learned the art of many moons ago while trying to make partner at Calhoun & Calhoun law offices. Until they closed the doors, that is. All the long hours and hard work hadn't done much good in the end, but this was a six-year-old, and being on time was still an important lesson.

His son came running down the hall, holding up one red sneaker, tears glistening in his eyes.

"I can't find my other sneaker," he said, his lower lip trembling ever so softly as he sniffed.

"Where did you leave it? One would think it couldn't be far from the one you're holding in your hand," Seth offered, trying to jog his son's memory.

"I looked, and I looked, but it's gone. I think a monster ate it, and now I can't go to school."

Suddenly, everything fell into place. This was Toby's attempt to stay home, his son having made no bones about the fact he wanted to stay home and help Seth. His rationale was in thinking he didn't need school when his dad could teach him everything he needed right there at the ranch. And yes, Seth could teach him about horses and ranching, but there were three problems that stopped him.

One, he too, needed a better knowledge of what was entailed in running an equine breeding ranch, especially given the terrible state of disrepair. Seth's experience had been through the eyes of a young boy, not a man running the place. And now, with the ranch used as collateral on a loan for the start-up expenses, everything was on the line. Failure was not an option.

Two, his son needed school learning. Teaching a first grader the core of an education that would compound over the years wasn't anything he was qualified to do.

And three, there was the little matter of time and patience...neither of which was a free-flowing commodity these days. "Let's look together," he said, taking his son by the hand to lead him back towards his bedroom.

The room was decorated in blues and reds with tiny splashes of yellow...Superman colors. It was the first room Seth had fixed up when they arrived at the ranch, hoping to help Toby settle in easier if he was surrounded by his favorite hero. Except there was nothing Superman-like about wanting to avoid school because he was afraid. Although, combined with unhappy, Seth was more than willing to give his son a pass. "Where did you find the one you are holding?"

"Right there," Toby said, pointing at an area of floor near the nightstand. "And I looked and looked, so it's no use. A monster got it. I just know it." The innocent look on his son's face didn't fool Seth, not in the least.

He glanced around the room but didn't spot the sneaker in any of the obvious spots. Near the bed, with Toby's toys, next to the pile of yesterday's clothes in the corner. Seth got down on his hands and knees and pulled a few toys out from under the bed. He glanced up at his son. "I thought we talked about how your toys should go in the toy box, not under the bed."

"Sorry, Daddy. I forgot," Toby added with a shrug.

Seth didn't believe him for a minute, especially since he had called him Daddy. Always trying to sound more grown up his son had started calling him Dad...except when he was in trouble. Toby was a normal child, wanting the quickest clean-up to get on with play time. Most likely, that entailed using his feet to shove the toys under the bed and declaring the job done. It was something Seth used to do, and something his mom and dad always caught onto...eventually. At least while they'd all been living together as a family. It hadn't taken Seth long to realize cleaning one's room took far longer when you wasted time trying to get out of the chore. In the end, Seth had learned his lesson. But then, that could have also been directly related to his dad's permanent departure from the family. An event that had scarred Seth deeply, but something he managed to hide from the world. Including his mother, as she had enough troubles on her own dealing with his dad's defection.

One more stuffed animal blocked his view, and when he pulled it aside, Seth spotted the bright red sneaker. He reached for it, scooted back, and held it up for inspection. "Got it. Wonder how it got so far under the bed?"

A guilty expression crossed Toby's face. "Might have been me. Do I really have to go to school?" he whined, hanging one last hope on the question.

"You do. I've got so much work to do to fix this place up for the two of us. You want a nice home, right?"

"Yes, sir," he mumbled.

"So do I. Which means I need to focus on restoring the horse ranch to the way your great-grandparents once had it in order to be profitable." The Dillinger Horse Ranch had been a top-notch breeder in the Equine Breeder's Association, and folks from all over the country traveled to Crossroads Creek to buy Dutch Warmbloods from them. A success Seth hoped to repeat.

"What's pro...fit...profitable?" Toby asked, sounding out the word.

"Making enough money for us to pay for what we need. Food, clothes, nights out at the movies. That sort of thing." It was a simplified version for a kid and Seth hoped it would do the trick to motivate his son to give the new school a chance. *One day at a time was his motto.*

"Okay, I'll go." Toby grumbled, swinging his one sneaker in the air by its laces. "But if I don't like it, promise me you'll come get me."

"I promise that the school will let you call me, and the rest we can discuss at that time. No sense getting into details about something that hasn't happened." The art of compromise was something else he learned at law school, and Seth found it useful in dealing with his son. He picked Toby up and sat him on the bed. Sliding the sneakers on his feet, Seth tied them both to save time, knowing his son hadn't mastered the bunny loops yet. Perhaps Velcro-strap sneakers were in order to speed up the morning process.

"Let's go," Seth said, helping Toby off the bed.

Hand in hand, they headed for the front door. He grabbed the lunchbox off the rustic, well-worn coffee table. It had been an original piece his grandfather made and one Seth wouldn't part with, no matter how much he fixed up the house. The wooden floorboards were another matter entirely as they were scuffed up and squeaky in places. Nothing some sanding and a fresh coat of stain couldn't fix.

"What if the other kids hate me?" Toby asked as he clicked on his seatbelt. "I wish I was back at my other school."

Toby's words ripped at Seth's heart, knowing all the changes had been brought about through no fault of his son. Only that he had the misfortune of having two parents who never loved each other in the first place. Parents who had their eyes and hope set on ambition and social status rather than on what was most important...Toby.

Something Seth was trying to change.

"What's not to love about you? You're a good kid, with a giant heart. And you've got Superman on your side." Seth ruffled his son's hair.

"I don't think Superman is allowed in school. They don't let strangers visit," Toby said, his down-to-earth practical side shining through.

"Well maybe just this once. I'll have a word with the principal," Seth said, shooting a smile at his son as he climbed into the truck. He drove to Parkview Elementary School, which was only seven minutes away. Parking in a front guest parking spot, they both exited the truck.

"Will you take me to my classroom?"

"Sure thing, buddy. Wouldn't dream of not seeing you off on your first day of school." Taking Toby by the hand, he led his son into the building.

"Good morning. You all must be new, seeing as I don't recognize you," a bright, cheery older woman with gray hair greeted them just inside the door.

"Yes, ma'am, we are. I'm Seth Dillinger, and this is my son, Toby. I've registered him for first grade already, but we're not sure where to go. Sorry if we're a little late. We had some sneaker trouble," he said, shooting his son a grin, hoping to ease his fears with humor.

"It's nice to meet you both. I'm Lori Jenson, one of the substitute teachers here. The first few days of school can be so exciting, and we never start on time, so don't worry about that one bit. Let me just check my list for you."

The woman glanced at her clipboard. "Ah, yes. Here you are," she said, checking off Toby's name. "You're in Miss Sullivan's classroom, and you will simply love her as a teacher," she said, smiling down at Toby. "Just go down the hall," she pointed, "turn right, and it's the first door on the left."

"Thank you," Seth said, hoping the woman knew what she was talking about. The sooner Toby fit in, the better it would be for Seth to be able to get more uninterrupted work hours in. So far, the balancing act between parenting and working on the ranch had been a lesson in futility.

Six months ago, he had no idea how much went into raising a child. Long hours spent trying to get ahead in life, paving the way for a better future, had gotten in the way of the present. Something he would rectify, even if it hadn't been by choice. No, that was all on the failed dream of making partner and the law firm closing its door. Topped with a sickening dose of Alicia, the ex-wife who suddenly recognized she wasn't willing to wait for the social status she sought and moved on—from both Seth and Toby.

"Oh, wait, I almost forgot," the woman called out as they moved off down the hall.

Seth stopped and turned as Lori Jenson rushed toward them.

"Let me get you a guest pass and a name tag for Toby. We find it encourages children to make friends faster when they know someone's name." She filled out the tags, handing one to Seth before she personally kneeled down and did the honors of pasting one on Toby's shirt. "There you go, young man. All set."

"Thank you, Miss Jenson. I did tell my son if for any reason he felt the need to call me, that you would allow him to do so. I hope that's not overstepping my bounds, but this is a new school, new town, new everything, and it's a bit overwhelming for Toby." Seth shot his son a smile as he honored this morning's promise.

The woman nodded. "Trust me, Mr. Dillinger, we understand. And of course he can call. We want school to be a fun place, and part of that is a feeling of security."

It was obvious the woman had been in education for many years, her sensitivity level and dedication to what was best for the children echoed in her words. "Thank you."

Toby clutched Seth's hand a little tighter as they headed down the hall. Standing at the door to the classroom, the buzz of excitement and flurry of activity all around the room was intriguing. Sea creatures adorned the walls, all bright, cheery, and fun. The letters of the alphabet and numbers had prominent spots in one corner where many bean bags were piled high, the rainbow of colors limitless.

Seth's gaze zeroed in on the older woman with gray hair, presumably Ms. Sullivan. She appeared to be nice enough, smiling as she handed out a pack of colors and several activity worksheets. Busy work to settle the children down would be his first guess.

But it was the assistant teacher who caught his eye and held his attention. Bright red hair, porcelain-like skin, and a smile that brought sunshine to the room. Her laughter rang out as she stopped and talked, moving from child to child and giving them each a hug. She reminded Seth of a bee going from flower to flower and spreading the sweet nectar.

A little girl came up to Toby, glared at his name tag, and then reached out her hand in greeting. "Hi, Toby. I'm Ava. You can sit next to me if you want, there's an empty seat."

Toby looked up at him and Seth nodded, hoping to encourage him to be brave.

"Thanks. I'm new here," Toby said.

"I know." Ava grinned and pointed at Toby's name tag. "I was new last year."

Seth kneeled next to his son and gave him a slight hug, unsure how a six-year-old felt about parental hugs in public. He had so much to learn. "I'll just let your teacher know what I told you and give her my number." Seth started toward the older woman, but Ava grabbed his arm.

"That's not the teacher. She's Miss Coble. *That's* Miss Sullivan over there," Ava said, quick to take charge and point him in the right direction.

"Okay, thanks." So the red-haired woman wasn't an assistant teacher after all.

Miss Sullivan spotted Toby instantly as he moved into the room and she rushed over to greet them, giving Toby a hug the same as Seth had seen her do with the other children. Warm and welcoming. He watched as the two talked a few moments before his son finally took his seat.

The teacher glanced in Seth's direction and headed his way. Her face was wreathed in the same smile she used on the kids. The woman didn't seem to have any other mode other than happy, reminding him of Mary Poppins.

"Hi there. I'm Leslie Sullivan, Toby's new teacher. It's nice to meet you Mr.—"

"Dillinger. Seth Dillinger." They shook hands, the softness of her skin in direct contrast with the firm handshake. Tough and un-yielding, but soft and comforting.

Leslie glanced back at Toby and then returned her attention to Seth. "Toby will do fine, I'll make sure of it personally."

"Thank you. He's not happy with having to come to a new school and all the other changes in his life, so I promised you'd let him call me if he needed to talk. I hope that wasn't an out-of-line promise."

Leslie shook her head. "Of course, it isn't. I love that you care and can be sensitive to his needs. But I can almost guarantee he won't be calling."

Seth quirked one eyebrow up in disbelief, her comment overly self-assured. "Based on?"

"Experience. I'm good with kids, Mr. Dillinger." Her confidence brooked no opposition.

He believed her. "Seth," he offered, feeling somewhat relieved. With Miss Sullivan in charge of Toby during school hours, Seth could concentrate on the ranch.

"Okay, then. I'm glad that's settled. And Leslie's fine. It's only the students who call me Miss Sullivan. I'll see you at three when you pick Toby up after school. The waiting line is outside, but I like to talk to the parents after the first day, especially with new students, or students that have a hard time adjusting back to school. I believe in a very open communication style between teachers and parents."

"Sounds good. See you then." Seth turned to leave just as another student came up to give her a hug. And just like that, he was forgotten. But there was nothing about Leslie's soft powder blue eyes he would forget anytime soon, as they reminded him of the Texas Bluebonnet's growing in the fields at the ranch.

His grandmother's favorite flower. Grace Dillinger had been the sweetest woman he had ever known, and the regret for not returning to visit her more often continued to linger. More so now that he had returned to the ranch and fond memories were close at hand.

Chapter Two

♥

As was her habit throughout the day, Leslie paid attention to each and every child. She tried to get a sense of the student's comfort zone and confidence levels, especially when she had a new kid in the school. A change in location and schools would have an element of emotional stress, and it remained to be seen how these changes had affected Toby Dillinger. Some kids did just fine. For others, they struggled to fit in. And from her own personal experience, that's where Leslie was cued up to help in any way possible.

The first day back at school was always a difficult one when it came to getting the children to settle in and direct their attention to learning.

Fun learning, but still education. Susan Coble, her assistant, had been teaching for over twenty years, and only recently dialed back her commitment to a teacher's assistant level. Leslie was more than a little grateful she'd chosen to help the first graders. The woman was a master at making sure the children had what they needed for each lesson, filler work, and she was the best at problem solving. Missing crayons. Missing lunches. Missing anything. And of course, potty breaks.

Which in turn left Leslie the opportunity to work creatively, filling the children's minds with their reading, writing, and arithmetic skills. Today, however, had been more about setting structure for the new first graders than any real teaching opportunity.

The door opened and Beth stuck her head in the door, scanned the room, and when she spotted Leslie, headed her way. Her best friend taught kindergarten, which was another reason Leslie was more cued into the first graders than most teachers would be with a new class.

Beth had a way of giving her the necessary updates on every child, her passion and caring for her students equal to Leslie's.

"What's up?" Leslie asked as a few of the children rushed up to give Beth a hug.

"I thought it would be fun to take the kids out to recess together and pull double time. What do you think?" Beth asked, all while never missing a beat as she hugged some of her students from last year.

"That's a great idea. I'll round the class up and meet you out on the playground."

"Yay," the girls standing next to them said.

"See you outside, Miss Thomas. I can't wait to tell you about my new kitten," Ava said.

"And I can't wait to hear seeing as I love cats." Beth turned and headed for the door.

Leslie faced the students and raised her hand for silence. "Quiet please, class. I've got a special treat to announce." She waited for the kids to calm down, eager anticipation on their sweet faces. "Most of you know Miss Thomas because she was your kindergarten teacher. She's asked us to join her class for recess so we will have double time outside to play."

"Yay," the class cheered.

"Let's clean up any of the papers you're working on and put the crayons back in the box, please," Susan called out as a reminder to the children, taking charge.

The level of chatter rose as they scurried to pick up their belongings in record time. Recess was always a great motivator. All except for Toby, that is. He hadn't moved out of his seat, his sullen glance flitting around the room. Once Susan had the children lined up at the door, Leslie started to move in Toby's direction. Just as she reached him, the boy made a move to stand up. Slow as a snail, he moved toward the back of the line.

Leslie took his hand and urged him to join the others as they continued out the door and down the hall. "We have a great playground here at Parkview, and I promise, you'll make friends quickly. For now, we can team up if you like.

Maybe kick a ball around a bit. The others are sure to join in."

Toby looked up at her, but his expression was unreadable. "Okay," he mumbled, not sounding overly confident, but obviously not willing to say no. Good manners were always a welcome commodity in the classroom.

"So, where did you move here from?" she asked, already knowing the answer but trying to draw him into conversation.

"L.A. It's a big city with lots of kids," Toby said.

Now they were getting somewhere. "I see. We have lots of kids too, even though we're a small town."

Toby shook his head, the frown he wore deepening. "But my friends aren't here. No one likes me."

It was the universal fear all children had...not fitting in. But it was how one handled it that made all the difference. "It takes time to make new friends, and you've got to be willing to try.

I'd say you're off to a great start for your first day."

"What do you mean?" he asked.

"Well, I'm your friend. And I saw Ava talking to you earlier. The next step is for you to talk to her. It shows common ground. She might have the impression you don't like her or want to be friends since you haven't said anything to her or anyone else all day. Did you ever think of that?" she asked gently, trying to get him to see that friendship was a two-way street.

"Nope." He shrugged.

"Why don't we go say hello? I'll be right beside you the whole time," she offered.

"I reckon." Toby's indifference was feigned, something her past had taught her to recognize. After all, she'd been a master at feigning emotion when she was his age.

They moved closer to where Ava and two of her friends were playing on the slide.

"Go on, say hi to Ava and the others," Leslie said, kneeling next to him until they were at the same level. Nudging him gently with her shoulder, she tried to prompt the initiative, knowing the kid's emotions would leave him feeling as though he were walking on a tightrope. A way across to the other side...but one wrong move and you fell. Which correlated with failure and would prompt him to regress even more deeply.

Leslie needed to do a little more digging into his records if she wanted to understand Toby more. And to jumpstart the process, she intended to talk to his father after school. A parent-teacher team could work wonders for a child's confidence and well-being if they worked together to make it happen.

Toby shuffled over closer to Ava, scuffing his feet in the sand with each step. Eyes downcast, he stopped short of the girls, but didn't say a word.

"Wanna play, Toby?" Ava asked.

"I guess," he said, eyes downcast.

"We take turns, but seeing as you haven't had one, why don't you go first?" Ava offered, pointing at the slide. The other girls nodded. "Hi, Toby. I'm Clarissa, and this is Lindsey. It's okay for you to go first, but get a move on, or I'm going." Clarissa laughed.

Toby finally looked up at the girls and nodded. "Well, okay then." He moved off toward the slide, grabbing the rail and climbing to the top, one rung at a time. Toby slid down...and landed on his backside. Close to tears, he stood and brushed the dirt off his pants, not looking at anyone.

Ava laughed, her friends joining in as they moved closer.

"Looks like you're okay, right Toby?" Ava asked, a smile at the ready.

Leslie might have stepped in to stop the girls from making a bad situation worse, but she also knew each one of them well enough to know the laughter wasn't meant with malice.

Toby glared at Ava, his pride getting in the way of a friendly response. He stormed off without a word and didn't even bother to return to Leslie's side for moral support. She watched as he headed for the swing set and claimed one of the swings. *Alone and in his own little world.*

Beth approached, and they moved more to the middle to keep a close eye on all the children. "What's up with the new kid?" her friend asked, nodding in Toby's direction.

"Divorced parents. New town. New school. All the issues one would expect him to be dealing with." Normal or otherwise, Leslie didn't like it.

"I hear a *but* in there somewhere," Beth countered.

"New kids have a sense of loss as they try to adjust, but Toby doesn't even act like he wants to adjust or fit in. I sense he would prefer to be left alone. There's just something about him that bothers me and I can't let it go." It was always this way when Leslie ran across a troubled child.

"It's a gift you have that goes beyond all understanding, and you shouldn't let it go. Trust in God and follow your instincts. You'll figure it out."

"But what if I'm wrong?" Leslie asked.

"You're never wrong. You've been through some special circumstances of your own when you were a kid and your perspective is a lot deeper, more emotional. Pray about it and I'm sure you'll find the answers to what makes him tick and how to help him come out of his shell. And even if you are wrong...isn't that a good thing?"

Beth had a point. She'd met her friend in college, and over the years the two of them had grown quite close. Beth was the only person Leslie had ever confided the truth of her childhood to, amongst other issues. "I hope you're right."

"And while you're at it...maybe you should find out more about the handsome cowboy I saw escorting Toby in the hall this morning. *Wowser,* is all I've got to say. That, and too bad his son wasn't five," she teased.

Leslie grinned and shook her head. "You're a hopeless romantic, but so off base."

"Give me one good reason you wouldn't want to have a parent-teacher conference with that guy," Beth said, bumping shoulders with her as she scanned the playground.

"That's easy and I'll give you three. One, he's recently divorced. Two, there's a rule against dating student's parents. And three, I'm not looking for a man." *And four...Beth was right...he was a good-looking cowboy.* How could she *not* notice his warm brown eyes with honey gold flecks, his strong angular jaw, or his athletic build? Not that she would admit that part to Beth.

Leslie didn't date, but it didn't mean she couldn't appreciate from afar.

Beth laughed. "So what? Rumor has it the man has been divorced long enough to start dating. Trust me, some of the other teachers are talking about it. The rumor mill in Crossroads Creek is alive and well. As for dating student's parents...there have been a few exceptions and no one seems to blink an eye. And as for you not looking...you should be. You're young, smart, beautiful, and wanting nothing more than a family of your own."

Leslie shook her head. "Those exceptions weren't anything like this situation. They were adults who were dating before the school year started and there were no other classrooms to move the child into. It really is for the best, as it can be detrimental to the student, and that's what's most important in all of this. As for the rest...I don't—"

Beth held up her hand. "Don't say another word. We've been friends for a long time and I know all your secrets. Secrets you told me, so I know them to be true."

Leslie let out a deep sigh. This was exactly why she avoided these types of conversations with her friend. "No guy who wants a real relationship would date someone who can't have kids and start a family. It's easier for them to find someone who can...just in case. And then what of me? The longing in my heart to hold a child of my own? I can't do that to myself. It's easier this way. Maybe when I'm forty and over the childbearing years," she added, shooting her friend a teasing glance, hoping to move on to safer subjects. This conversation was way too deep for the playground.

"The right guy would date you no matter whether you could have kids or not. Lots of people nowadays choose not to have kids. It's all about trusting someone not to break your heart. Your perfect someone is out there, but if you don't try to find him, you never will."

Beth walked away, leaving Leslie alone with her thoughts. Her friend was right but it didn't instill any confidence for Leslie to put herself out there and risk getting hurt. *Again.* Once was enough with Brad. Not to mention she had plenty of friends she could trust, her life richer and more grounded than if she had a man in her life who could hurt her.

Then why are you trying to get Toby to put himself out there? The thought came out of nowhere, but Leslie knew it came straight from God.

Luckily, she had the no-dating-parent's rule to fall back on.

Chapter Three

SETH HAMMERED THE NAIL in place, shoring up the barn loft beams with new 2x10 trusses. He wiped the sweat off his forehead with the sleeve of his shirt. Glancing at his watch, he shook his head, and tossed the hammer next to the stack of wood and box of nails. At this pace, it would take him a year to get the horse ranch up to speed and fully stocked with quality breeding mares and a stallion. The goal from the minute he'd seen the place, run down and devoid of all that made the place special when he was a boy, had been to restore the ranch to its former glory. His grandparents had left him the place because they believed in Seth, trusting him with their legacy.

When he inherited the ranch, Seth had been in full swing vying for the title of partner at the law firm where he had worked right after college, not to mention, married and with a newborn to consider. He had done the only thing he could do...hire someone to sell the horses and close the ranch down.

The other choice had been to sell...something he could never bring himself to do, much to the chagrin of his now ex-wife, Alicia. She hated the place almost as much as he loved it. And now, in a strange twist of fate, he was living here with Toby. Not selling, it turned out, had been providential. And once Seth had a chance to mull over the books he had found boxed up and stashed away in one of the guest bedroom closets, he had a far better understanding of what needed to be done. More importantly, who to do business with. Reputable contacts and connections were the crux of an equine breeding business if one wanted to be successful.

Six years was a long time in the business world and lots of things could change...the expenses involved being one of them. Research had quickly shown him that while expenses had almost doubled over the years, the price for foals had only increased by twenty-five percent. The key was to streamline the operation.

The decision to put the ranch up as collateral hadn't been an easy one but was necessary if he wanted to give the ranch a chance to succeed. At fifteen to twenty thousand dollars to breed a mare and care for the foal, it was an all or nothing venture. But with his grandparents' detailed notes, Seth's desire to succeed, and hopefully, his ability to pick the right mares from the beginning would dictate the future of the ranch. That, and Seth's determination to find a stallion in the direct lineage of Lloyd Dillinger's prized stallion, Octavius Stargazer.

Seth's biggest regret was not getting back to see his grandparents much after his own parents split, but now, he had a chance to do right by his grandparents and the horse ranch they'd poured their heart and soul into.

Seth's parents should have inherited the place, or at the very least, his father, after they were divorced. But Grace and Lloyd Dillinger had never forgiven their son for deserting his family, and by extension Seth's mother was also to blame. His father had ghosted them when he was six, the man not seen or heard from since, and his mother had remarried and had a new family that occupied her attention, leaving Seth pretty much on his own to make his way in the world.

And now, he was starting over. A chance to press the reset button on his life and make things right for Toby. To do that, he first had to get the ranch up and running and breed foals of the same high quality and characteristics as his grandparents had once done. This was his proving ground of sorts. Add to that his plan to offer foaling services for other breeders, and Seth fully believed the ranch could be successful.

Everything would depend on the first two mares and a miracle...they both needed to get pregnant on the first attempt, as stud fees and vet expenses were quite high. Luckily, starting tomorrow, Claudia Mitchell, his closest neighbor, had agreed to help watch Toby and cook dinners, freeing up even more of Seth's time.

He drove to the school and pulled into the pickup line, hoping to make short work of the process. If he was lucky, he could find something for Toby to do in the barn for a few hours. A chore that would change the kid's mind about school and make his son happy to leave the hard work to his father come morning.

A group of kids stood off to one side, Seth spotting his son standing sullenly next to the assistant teacher. Leslie and her unmistakable flaming red hair headed in his direction. She rested her arms on the driver's side window before he realized her destination.

"Good afternoon, Seth," she said, a smile touching her freckled face.

Seth nodded, tipping his hat ever so slightly. "Afternoon. Is there a problem? I see Toby, but he's not headed this way. I'm kind of in a hurry."

Leslie didn't seem the least bit rattled by his declaration and the hint to leave. "I asked Susan to keep him occupied a few minutes to give me a chance to have a private word with you."

"Okay. So what's going on? Did Toby do something wrong?" He resigned himself to another short delay.

"No, not at all. It's what he's not doing that concerns me," she said.

Seth let out a sigh of relief. "What's that supposed to mean?"

"Toby's had a rough day, and I'm worried about him. He's not willing to interact with the other kids, or even willing to try. He seems lost in his own world, and I'm not one to let things slip by. It's important to me to make sure children get the proper attention when something isn't right in their world."

"I see, and I appreciate your concern. Toby would have preferred to stay home with me today and help out on the ranch. I'd say that's fairly normal. I mean, it is school. And it's his first day in a new school and new town, so it's to be expected. Give him a few days and he'll adjust." At least Seth hoped he would, especially with Claudia keeping an eye on him after school. The elderly woman might be precisely what Toby needed. Someone to pay him more attention while he settled in. There just wasn't enough time in the day for Seth to do everything and be everywhere. Not if he wanted the house ready for winter.

"You're probably right, but I'm not sold on that theory yet. At least not as the sole cause. And the result of not making certain can end up becoming emotionally harmful to a child," Leslie said, her voice low but urgent.

Except Seth didn't need the teacher psychoanalyzing Toby's behavior—that was his job. A job he took seriously, even if he was new at it. Alicia had taken care of all Toby's needs right up until the day she left them both...for someone new. "Thanks for your insights, and

I promise I'll talk to him about this. I'm sure you're aware his mother and I are divorced, and it's possible he's still upset about it even though it was six months ago," Seth said by way of dismissal.

Without so much as a backward glance, Alicia had given up parental rights to Toby, both physical and legal, all for the promise of fun and social status with a new man in her life. Talk about selfish, not to mention something that had blindsided Seth, coming on the heels of the law firm closing...it had all been overwhelming. He was doing his best, even if Toby's teacher didn't see it that way.

"That would be great. And I'll keep a close eye on him in school. If you figure anything out, please let me know. Parent-teacher teams can be a lifesaver for children trying to work through issues or adjust to changes."

"I'm sure that won't be necessary. I'm his father and I feel certain we can work through this at home," he said, trying to dispel her attitude that he needed help to raise Toby. Although he truly did need help at times, he would be the last person to admit it, or accept it. Because so far, trusting others didn't seem to work out for him. Not as a child, and certainly not as an adult.

Leslie's gentle smile faded, her lips pursed ever so slightly. For some reason, she took offense at his rejection, but it wasn't his problem. Toby was his only concern, and his pretty teacher wouldn't change that reality.

She moved away from the truck and signaled for Susan to send Toby on his way. His son's slumped shoulders and withdrawn taut facial features struck him hard in the heart. So much for Seth's hope that Toby would make friends and begin to fit in. The two of them would talk, although what he would say, Seth didn't have a clue. He had no experience when it came to this sort of thing. *Emotional things.*

Toby climbed in the truck and Seth double checked his seatbelt before climbing back in the driver's seat. "Did you have a good day at school, buddy?"

"Nope. Told you I shouldn't have gone," Toby said, his voice sullen.

With a quick glance back at the school, he spotted Leslie. Seth shook his head and drove off. Her help might have been a blessing, but he couldn't trust her. Couldn't trust anyone. Not anymore. And especially not with Toby.

He'd find a way to break through and figure out what was going on in his son's head and figure out what to do about it. *On his own.* "Tell me what happened?"

"Nothing," his son mumbled.

"There had to be something, so let's talk about it." Seth glanced in the rear-view mirror as he drove to the ranch. Toby's hard expression hadn't changed one bit.

"Just some dumb girls laughing at me, and none of my friends in L.A. to play with. School was boring and I don't want to go back. I told you I would hate it."

Seth shook his head. "We've talked about this. School is necessary to learn things you need to know to help you get smart as you grow up. And it's the law."

"You can teach me. John Phelps' mom used to teach him at home, and nobody said a thing. And he's smart."

Leave it to Toby to remember his friend and their situation. "John's mother was a stay-at-home mom, and she was well qualified to teach her children. I have to work at the ranch and I can't do both, son. I'm sorry. I do have some good news though...Mrs. Mitchell has agreed to watch you after school. She'll pick you up and take you to her place next door starting tomorrow. She also watches her granddaughter, so you'll have someone your age to play with." Seth was grasping at straws, but it was all he had.

Toby huffed. "Play with a girl? Girls are boring."

Seth shook his head, his frustration mounting. "Girls can be just as much fun as a boy. It's all in how you look at it."

"What's her name?" his son asked, taking Seth by surprise.

"I think she said Ava something or other."

"No way," Toby said, shaking his head. "I don't want to go there. I want to come home and work with you. Please, Daddy."

His son's voice had taken on a slight whine he couldn't fail to miss, putting Seth on red alert. "Do you know this girl?"

"Yup. She's one of the girls that pretended to be nice and then laughed at me when I fell at the bottom of the slide. Mean girls," he said, scrunching up his face.

Toby was one of those kids who acted much younger than his age when he didn't get his way or was upset about something. In other words, normal for a six-year-old boy. "Did you get hurt?" Seth asked.

"No." Toby pouted.

"I've seen you laugh at yourself and shrug it off when you land wrong before. So what's different about this time?" It had been one of those rare occasions Seth took a Sunday off and they'd gone to the park. Toby had been showing off, perhaps to impress Seth, but he'd laughed it off like it was all planned.

"They laughed *at* me. I think it was mean."

Seth understood, or at least he thought he did. "Maybe they wanted to laugh to make you realize it was no big deal and help you through the awkwardness. Laughing doesn't have to be mean spirited." It was easy to take offense when your injured pride was on the line.

"That's what Miss Sullivan told me. And that girl Ava did ask if I was okay, so maybe you are right. I just hated that I looked stupid in front of them."

And there lay the root of the issue. "Landing on your backside and not getting hurt is funny, not stupid. It's something all kids and even grownups have happen once in a while, yourself included. Try to keep that in mind, Toby."

"Maybe. But not everyone does it on their first day at a new school," Toby was hanging on to his injured pride with every last ounce of determination.

A trait he got from Seth. "You have a point, but it's all good and behind you. You won't have another first day at a new school until middle school."

Toby shrugged. "I guess. I like my new teacher. Miss Sullivan was really nice to me."

It would seem the moment was over. Seth took great satisfaction in the fact that by talking to his son, they had gotten through this little hiccup. Proof Seth could do it on his own. "That's great." Of course his son liked Miss Sullivan. She was pretty, friendly, and was clearly dedicated to her job.

"She tried to help me make friends today, but I don't want new friends. I want my old friends." Toby pouted.

It had been a check in the win column, even if for a short period. "You have to let go of the past and move forward, son. We live here now."

"Miss Sullivan helped me pick up my things and pack my bag to come home. She said I could talk to her anytime I needed to or if I had questions."

Seth nodded. "That's good." It sounded like Leslie had focused on Toby most of the day, perhaps to the neglect of the other students.

"*Bit of a busybody if you ask me,*" Seth mumbled under his breath.

Chapter Four

♥

TOBY'S ATTITUDE WASN'T IMPROVING, despite Leslie's attempts to draw him into various small groups of children as they worked on their activities. He kept to himself, working solo, ignoring the other kids. Not that she didn't see him sneak peaks on occasion at what the other kids were drawing.

Leslie moved to stand next to him, curious about his picture. The artistic ability was typical of a first grader, an age when pictures became more realistic, colorful, and creative. It was one of the many things she loved about this age group as they learned to fine tune their motor skills and started to draw pictures based on stories or something they'd seen or loved.

"Don't forget to put your name on your paper, Toby," she said, leaning over him and pointing to the blank space. It was the third time she had to remind him today.

Toby paused, looked up at her. "Sorry." He moved his hand to the top of the page and scrawled his name in capital letters. Legible at best, but then he hadn't put any real effort into making it look nice.

Now wasn't the time to comment on neatness. "Thank you. Can you tell me about your picture?" she asked, trying to engage Toby in a conversation. It was always more fun to hear the children tell their own story.

Toby shrugged. "Not much. It's just me and my dad."

"I see. So this must be your house...and your dog. What's his name?" she said, pointing as she spoke.

"I don't have a dog. I wish I had one, but my dad tells me no every time I ask." The forlorn expression on his face deepened.

"There's nothing wrong with a pretend dog. Do you have a name for him?" she encouraged, hoping to help him open up and talk.

"Gabe. That was my best friend's name back in California. I miss him."

Leslie nodded. "That's a great name. And I'm sure you'll meet new best friends here if you give the other kids a chance."

Toby shrugged again.

His indifference was concerning, and Leslie was determined to keep a special eye on him and help him make the adjustment. Not just because it was part of her job, but mostly because she didn't want him to fall through the cracks the way she had when she was a little older than he was now.

"What's a busybody?" he asked suddenly.

"Where on earth did you learn that word?" Leslie grinned at him, the question coming out of nowhere and catching her off guard.

"My dad."

Interesting. "I see. A busybody is a person who likes to get into other people's business."

"So are you one? A busybody, I mean," Toby asked, the innocence of his question softening the sting.

"I hope not. It's not generally considered a good quality," Leslie said, trying to clarify the meaning a bit more.

"I need to tell my dad he's wrong then, cause he called you a busybody."

Seth Dillinger had a lot to learn about parenting young children, and about people in general. One, you didn't say anything you didn't want a child to repeat. Two, he was wrong about her. There was a difference between a busybody and someone who cared enough to help when needed.

Not that she'd share all that with Toby, because unlike Seth, she knew better.

"Miss Sullivan, look at what I drew?" Monica waved her drawing in the air from across the table.

"It's beautiful. I love colorful flowers. Can you tell me what it means to you?" Leslie asked, moving to her side.

'That's me and Lindsey playing on the swings in the park. She's my new best friend. Look how high we can go?" Monica looked up, her eyes shining with excitement as she proudly shared her drawing.

"It's lovely. And yes, you've gone quite high. High enough to see over the treetops. Like a giant," Leslie added with a grin.

"Yeah. It's just pretend though. We can't really swing that high," Monica confided.

"True, but it's okay to pretend. Toby's got a pretend dog in his drawing." Leslie offered up the information, hoping to draw the two kids into a conversation together. Compare notes.

"I have a real dog," Monica said, her smile widening. "His name is Lucky."

Leslie nodded. "That's a wonderful name. And I bet there's a great story that goes with it."

"We adopted him from the animal shelter and my mom said, *that's one lucky dog*. She didn't want a dog, but I promised to take good care of him and help out. The name Lucky stuck, I guess. What's your dog's name, Toby?" Monica asked.

Leslie smiled, pleased the young girl remembered to ask him.

"Nothing. It's a stupid pretend dog," Toby said as he began scratching out the dog on the paper.

Leslie was at a loss for what to say. Every chance Toby had of connecting, he pulled away. And he grew more sullen.

"Okay, class...just a few more minutes to finish up your drawings and then we will go to the lunchroom. Leave your artwork on your desk and I'll collect them after you leave with Miss Coble."

Excitement filled the room as lunchtime brought social time, followed by more social time on the playground. Something every child enjoyed. *Except perhaps Toby.*

Ten minutes later, the quiet of the classroom gave her time to eat her own lunch and go through all the morning lessons turned in. One by one, she went through each stack, checking over the answers. There were always mistakes in math. She smiled at one paper where two apples plus two apples made ten apples, the student clearly carried away with drawing apples and coloring them in, each one a different color.

When she came to Toby's paper, however, his answers almost seemed intentionally wrong. The pictures of fruit were always correct, it was the written answer that was always wrong. Leslie put a smiley face on the top to show he'd finished the page, simply listing the correct answers for reference. It's not as though Leslie graded the papers, using them mostly to teach, and helping children understand and learn how to follow directions, easing them into the expectations of schoolwork. It was something she would have to ask him about, as this wasn't a pattern that could continue for long without intervention. The last thing she wanted was for Toby to fall behind in school.

She continued through the rest of the papers and moved on to the drawings her assistant teacher had collected. The assignment had been to draw something fun about your life. There was a wide variety of families, pets, friends, and a few with Christmas and all the presents under the tree. And then there was Toby's. Leslie knew he'd crossed out the dog, but what she saw now was even more concerning. The page had clearly been crumpled and Toby had added large teardrops to the face of the little boy in the picture. Whether Seth Dillinger agreed or not, his son wasn't making the adjustment to his new life easily and he needed special attention before it got any worse.

Leslie glanced at her watch. It was time to take the children out to the playground and let Susan have her lunch break. Stacking all the papers, they would be handed back out for each child to take home. Holding back Toby's paper, she planned to share it with his father after school, hoping to make her point.

"Everything go okay?" she asked, joining her assistant where the children were lined up next to the wall, ready to go outside. Excitement filled the air, the kids keyed up for playtime.

"Perfect. They're all yours," Susan said, smiling as she glanced at the class.

"Let's go, children. Try to keep your voices down as we pass the other classrooms," she reminded them.

"Yes, Miss Sullivan," several of the children called out.

The minute they were outdoors, some tore off running for the playground, while others headed for the container of soccer balls and jump ropes, and Leslie's personal favorite...the skip bell. It was a toy she herself had used on many occasions as a way to self-entertain. When she started teaching, it had been a surprise to discover the toy was still around, and on a few silly occasions, she tried to make use of it...without much success.

Spying Toby by the monkey bars, Leslie moved to talk to him, hoping to gain some insight as to what upset him enough to make the changes he had to his drawing. Ava reached

Toby first and Leslie paused, wanting to see the interaction. She edged closer.

"Why aren't you playing with us? Don't you like us?" Ava asked bluntly, her face scrunched up in a frown and hands on her hips.

Toby scowled. "Play with you? Why would I do that?"

"I thought we were friends," Ava said, standing her ground.

"You laughed at me when I fell at the bottom of the slide. That was mean," Toby said, scuffing his foot on the rubber playground chips and sending a few flying.

Ava smiled. "Is that all? It was to make you feel better. My mom says laughter is the best medicine. That's why I asked if you got hurt when you didn't laugh with us."

"I felt stupid," Toby said, but at least he was still talking and hadn't stormed off.

"But we all fall. Haven't you ever fallen before?" Ava asked.

"Well, yeah," he mumbled.

Ava smiled. "So are we friends?"

"I guess." Toby shrugged.

"Cool. Want to swing with me?"

"Sure."

And just like that, Toby had his first friend.

Seth Dillinger could learn a thing or two from his son.

Chapter Five

♥

THURSDAY ROLLED IN AND still, the changes in Toby weren't enough to give Leslie the warm fuzzies, not even in the slightest. And as to her student's father, she hadn't seen or heard from Seth since the first day. He had hired Claudia, one of the sweetest elderly ladies in Crossroads Creek, to watch Toby after school. Mrs. Mitchell was also Leslie's friend, but it didn't mean she would discuss Toby's situation with the woman. That was a private conversation intended for his father. Eventually, she'd catch up with Seth.

Leslie lined up the children, two in a row, at the door, ready to walk them to the car pool waiting area where they were scheduled for pickup. The buzzing vibration of her phone in her back pocket startled Leslie. Most people knew not to call during school hours and she fully expected it to be a spam call. A quick glance revealed her guess was incorrect.

Claudia Mitchell.

Most odd, especially given Leslie had just been thinking about the woman. Perhaps Claudia's ears had been ringing. Leslie smiled, but clicked the button to receive the call, worry settling in the pit of her stomach like a lead weight. "Good afternoon, Claudia. What's up?"

"Oh, thank goodness you answered," Claudia said in a rush.

"What's wrong? Are you okay?"

"I'm just fine. It's my sister. She fell and broke her ankle and I've got to go stay with her in Dallas for a few weeks. Her grandchildren are visiting and I need to take over, seeing as the oldest is only nine."

Leslie frowned. "I'm so sorry to hear about her accident. I'll keep your sister in my prayers for sure. When are you planning to leave?"

she asked, her gaze landing on Toby. Claudia should have already been here at the school to pick him up.

"I'm packing as we speak. If I leave now, I can be there by suppertime. But there's Toby to consider and I haven't been able to reach his father to let him know the change in plans. I can't leave Seth high and dry...but that's where you come in."

"Me? How so?" The direction of this conversation had just taken a personal turn somehow.

"You're Toby's teacher and he trusts you. And Seth knows you. The whole town knows how good you are with your students. Can you please, please take care of Toby after school while I'm gone? It will only be for a couple of weeks, I promise."

The light clicked on...but Claudia didn't understand what she was asking Leslie to do. "I'm not sure his father would approve of the change." In fact, she was positive the man *wouldn't* approve. The term busybody came to mind, furthering Leslie's assessment of the situation and Seth's opinion of her.

"He's simply trying to be a good dad and can be a bit overbearing at times. The man has a good heart, and he loves his son and wants what's best for him. Trust me on this. And what's best for Toby right now would be for you to watch him. It's ideal if you ask me. You can take him to the ranch after school and then be home by dinner. Everyone's happy."

Claudia was trying to sell her on the plan and it sounded workable, but not idyllic. There was Jelly to consider, for starters. The dog needed to go outside right after school. And there was still Seth to consider. As for Toby, it would be fine as it could be the opening Leslie needed to bond more with the child, figure out what was bothering him, and find a way to help. "I don't know." It was a big decision to make at such short notice.

"Please, Leslie. I promise it will all work out, and I'll make sure to leave Seth a message and explain everything."

Claudia's persistence was wearing her down. "Okay, then. I'll do it. For Toby, you, and your sister." But not for Seth. *Busybody indeed.*

"Thank you. You're such a blessing to everyone in this town. I've got to call my sister and let her know I'm on my way," Claudia said, the gratitude in her voice unmistakable.

"Don't—"

"Bye."

"Forget to call Seth," Leslie mumbled into the phone, even though the call had been disconnected.

The school bell rang, reminding Leslie of her other duties. "Class, let's stay in line and make our way to the carpool area. Anyone not on the list to be picked up today, follow Mrs. Thompson out to the bus. And make sure to share your lessons and drawings with your parents when you get home. You've all worked hard and should be proud of yourselves."

Some of the kids waved and shouted good bye as Susan led them down the hall in a different direction.

Leslie kneeled next to Toby. "Mrs. Mitchell had to leave town in an emergency and she's asked me to look after you in her absence. Would that be okay with you?"

Toby shrugged. "I guess."

The indifference was in gesture and in words, but he wasn't able to hide the sudden glimmer of excitement shining in the depths of his warm brown eyes. Proof that Claudia was right...this would be a good thing for Toby. And if it was right for Toby, it was right for Leslie...as it would also give her time to check out the home situation. It would also allow her to get to know Seth better, perhaps even give him some pointers on how best to help Toby. What father wouldn't want that kind of help?

The Seth Dillinger kind.

Leslie led the children outside, and one by one, she said her goodbyes, helping the students into their parent's vehicle, and making sure all seatbelts were firmly locked into place.

"Thanks for waiting so patiently, Toby. I'll take you home now, but if you don't mind, I need to stop by my house for a minute to let the dog out."

Toby gazed up at her and smiled. "You have a dog?"

"I do. Her name is Jelly."

"That's a weird name for a dog," Toby said, his sudden smile like a ray of sunshine.

"Well, her real name is Lady Anastasia Sullivan, but that's a mouthful. And when she nabbed a piece of toast off the table and got jelly all over her face...the nickname stuck."

Toby scrunched up his face in distaste. "That must have been so messy."

Leslie nodded, reminded of Jelly's mad dash around the house to evade getting washed up, and managing to make more of a mess for her to clean up. Including the sofa. "It was, but I love her just the same."

"So even if she does bad things, you love her?" he asked.

Strange question from a six-year-old. "Of course. Love shouldn't be conditional."

"I want to meet Jelly." Toby's thoughtful expression bothered her, but he'd changed the subject, letting the conversation drop.

They walked to the car, and it wasn't long before they were pulling into the driveway. The small cottage was a welcome sight, with all the fall flowers in bloom and butterflies dancing in the air as they flitted from flower to flower. Leslie liked to think of it as her place of peace. "Don't let Jelly jump on you. She gets a bit excited when I get home, especially with someone new to check out," Leslie warned.

Toby shook his head. "I don't mind. I love dogs." He stopped halfway up the path. "Your house is kind of small, isn't it?"

"Yes, but it's more than enough space for just me and Jelly." Leslie opened the door, and her faithful canine rushed outside to greet the newcomer. Within seconds, dog and boy were playing in the front yard, where a game of chase had ensued.

Leslie sat down on the porch to watch, having been forgotten in the excitement. She loved hearing Toby's genuine laughter.

"I love Jelly," Toby called out just as he landed on the ground and rolled over to play with the dog. "She's got floppy brown ears that are so soft."

"She's a mixed breed dog, but mostly beagle. Or at least I think she is because of her ears," Leslie said, grinning at the pair as they played. She'd adopted Jelly at from the animal shelter and they didn't have much information on the dog, but Leslie had been all too willing to take a chance on the sweet puppy with soulful eyes.

"Cool. Someday, my dad said I could have a dog and I want one just like Jelly," Toby announced.

If a dog could bring out this much joy in the child, it was certainly something his father should consider. After all, the changes in Toby's life weren't his fault, and sometimes a child needed something new and positive in their life to offset negative change. "Well, for now, we can stop by here every day after school until Mrs. Mitchell returns and you can play with Jelly. How's that sound?"

"Sounds super-duper to me." Toby took off running after the dog.

For the next fifteen minutes, the two practically forgot Leslie existed. But it was long enough for Leslie to go over and over in her head what to say to Seth. The man might not want advice, but he was going to get some anyway.

Chapter Six

❤

SETH PULLED THE TRUCK and trailer up close to the barn and unloaded the two Dutch Warmbloods he'd bought in Wylie from a thoroughbred ranch. The two mares stood at sixteen and seventeen hands respectively and were of a beautiful sleek grey coloring with black manes. The white marks on their heads and lower legs were typical of the breed. Strong, athletic horses with a bloodline that had been blessed with many well-known show jumpers. Their bloodlines included several outstanding show jumpers and therefore they came with a hefty price tag. Hopefully, for his sake, one of their qualities included a highly fertile gene.

The timing wasn't ideal considering most foaling was targeted for the summer and they would be a little later than that if everything went well. Knowing the mares had already been prepped for breeding with special nutrient rich feed and vaccines, Seth made the rancher an offer he couldn't refuse knowing how important it was to get things rolling.

So far he hadn't found a stallion he would invest big bucks in, and Seth decided there was no choice but to resort to artificial insemination this first time around, though his grandfather preferred a sire.

Based on the cost of the entire process, Seth could afford to go all in this time, but after that, there was no way to keep everything going. Not when it would mean the difference of losing the ranch altogether or keeping the house as a roof over their heads and Seth going back to work in town to pay the current mortgage.

The dream was to fill the barn to capacity, perhaps fifteen to eighteen horses in all. His grandparents always had at least a dozen, but often, it was more than that. And with a couple of foaling stalls, and the ability to provide a foaling service for other breeders, he'd be in business and carrying on the legacy of his grandparents. But it all started with these first two mares he had chosen and the ability to multiply the stock.

The ride home had taken longer than he expected because, between his GPS system and spotty service, there had been several missed turns and dead-end back roads. Never a good thing when it came to towing a trailer and valuable horses.

Luckily, Claudia put up with his odd hours and had let him know she would be fine staying later that evening. After making sure each horse was secured in their stall, he added fresh water to the trough, and a small amount of feed. He took a few minutes to bond with each horse, talking gently to them and with a flat palm offered each one a carrot, hoping to reassure them. "I'll give you both time to get settled in and will be back to check on you in a few hours."

After Toby had gone to bed. A cowboy's work was never done...something his body knew all too well as of late.

It's not that he hadn't worked out while living in L.A. The gym was a regular part of his routine during lunch hour, but this was another story entirely. Ranching used muscles he didn't even know he had, and the long hours went way beyond the sixty-hour work weeks at the office. It was hard work, yes, but Seth had to admit, somewhat fulfilling. A new challenge that occupied most of his time, both mentally and physically.

Even the evenings were no rest for the weary as he pored over his grandfather's notes in the journals he had found. Luckily, Lloyd Dillinger had been methodical in the entries, and they were more than enough to guide Seth.

Exiting the barn, he made a beeline for the house. Driving around the side extension that led to the barn, he hadn't seen the strange car parked out front. His curiosity went into overdrive, given it wasn't Claudia's vehicle and hers was nowhere to be seen. After her granddaughter was picked up, the plan had been for her to come to the ranch to help get Toby settled in for the evening.

Taking the front porch steps in two strides, he reached for the screen door and pulled it open. "Claudia? Toby?" he called out, stepping inside, trying to quell the sudden sense of unease.

Toby came running down the hallway. "Dad, you're home. You were gone a long time today."

Seth was relieved to see his son and know everything was okay. "Sorry, kiddo. Work took me a long way from home. But wait until you see what I bought." He smiled at his son, knowing all would be forgiven when he heard the news.

Toby's eyes widened into big saucers. "A dog. You got me a dog? Really?" Toby asked, joy radiating from every inch of his body.

So maybe it wasn't the best thing for his son, but it was still quite exciting. "No, nothing like that. We've talked about that and we're not ready to take on the responsibility. I did, however, buy two horses."

His son's elated expression dropped a notch or two. Or three. A few seconds later, his smile was back in place. "Oh, I get it. A horse for me, and a horse for you. That's so cool."

Seth shook his head. "Sorry, they aren't pets. More like working horses as they are the first of the mares we need to breed. Vet's coming first thing in the morning. All part of the plan to get the ranch up and running."

Toby's smile slid into a frown, his shoulders slumped. "So we have horses that can't be ridden. That figures. I wish we were back in L.A.," he mumbled.

"Not exactly. The horses need exercise, but neither one of these mares are your size and you have to learn how to ride first. That won't happen on an expensive horse, or a pregnant one for that matter." The facts of life weren't always easy for a child to accept, but there was no other way to break the news.

"I get it. No dog. No horse. No nothing. But Miss Sullivan has a dog, and Jelly is so sweet. She loves me as much as I love her."

Seth did a double take as Toby's words sank in. "And how do you know all this? And where's Miss Mitchell?" he asked, his forehead drawn tight as he tried to make heads or tails of what was going on. Claudia still hadn't shown up and he didn't know whose vehicle was parked out front.

"He knows because we stopped at my house to let Jelly go potty before we came to the ranch. And it's a good thing we did considering how late—"

"Leslie? What are you doing here?" Seth asked, spinning around as he recognized the voice coming from behind him.

Leslie stopped short, one hand to her chest. "Oh, my. Claudia said she would leave you a message and explain everything. Please tell me she called you."

Seth shook his head. "No message," he said, holding up his phone to emphasize the point.

"Miss Sullivan is gonna watch me after school cause Mrs. Mitchell's sister busted up her ankle. Isn't that right?" Toby asked his teacher for confirmation.

Seth held up his hand. "Wait one minute. Leslie, do you mind telling me what's going on? In a way I can understand." When he left this morning, it never crossed his mind everything back home would get turned upside down in his absence.

"Toby's basically got it right," she said with a shrug. "Claudia's sister did break her ankle. She needed to leave immediately to help her sister with the visiting grandkids and asked me to fill in for her and take care of Toby after school until she returned. It's just temporary and Claudia was supposed to leave you a message. Maybe she got caught up in the situation and forgot. I'm sorry you didn't know before this, but Toby's safe with me. Something Claudia knew since I was already his teacher and Toby already knows and trusts me."

"I see." He didn't, but it was starting to fall into place. Seth had to agree with Claudia's judgement in an emergency situation, and that the busybody teacher probably was the best choice. Not to mention, he would have had great difficulty finding a replacement on such short notice.

Surely he could put up with Toby's teacher for a day or two. "So will she be back Monday before Toby gets out of school?" Seth asked, trying to get all the pieces back into place.

"Nope. Miss Sullivan's gonna watch me for two whole weeks. And I get to play with Jelly every day after school. She said so. Ain't that right?" Toby asked, more sure of himself.

"Isn't that right?" Seth corrected before turning to Leslie. "Two weeks?" *No way.*

Leslie nodded. "That's what Claudia said. I hope this isn't a problem for you. Otherwise, you'll need to find someone else."

Her matter-of-fact tone meant Leslie was all too aware he didn't know anyone in town. At least not well enough to ask them to watch his son and basically take over his home during his absence. "We both know that's not an option."

"Miss Sullivan and I were playing a folding clothes game when you got here. I was winning." Toby beamed. "She's the best."

"Funny, but you won't fold clothes when I ask you to," Seth said, glancing from Toby to Leslie, a frown etched on his face. Folding clothes was never considered fun...not when he was growing up, and certainly not now that he was responsible for everything that got dirty. Seth acknowledged a small nugget of respect for Leslie, at least to himself. Wouldn't do any good to give her ideas that her interference in his affairs was needed.

Leslie grinned. "That's because it's normally work. This is play."

"We try to see who can fold the best and the smallest and the most in one minute. And I'm really good at socks and shirts," Toby announced, pride reflected in his voice. "We still need to finish, Miss Sullivan." His son started toward the hall.

Leslie shook her head. "I finished up when you ran out to meet your dad, so our game is over and I declare you the winner." She shot Toby a warm smile.

A flicker of jealousy passed through Seth, his son's adoration of the woman obvious. Leslie could do fun and games, but he was Toby's father. What about all the fun and games they had together? The thought caught him off guard. There hadn't been much time for fun things lately with all that needed to be done on the ranch.

Who was he kidding? Before Alicia left, Seth had always been at the office trying to make partner...all for the good of the family. Wasted time as far as he was concerned now. "It's getting late. Have you eaten yet, Toby?"

"Yup. We had tomato soup and yummy grilled cheese sandwiches. Miss Sullivan knows how to make the cheese ooey-gooey."

More adoration for the teacher that Seth could do without. "That's cool. Glad to hear you ate though, seeing as it's about bedtime. And I need to fix my own dinner still."

"Bedtime? But—"

"No buts. It's a school night and Miss Sullivan has to get home. I'm sure she has things to do there, like walking her dog."

"Okay," Toby mumbled. "Bye, Miss Sullivan. See you at school on Monday." His son headed down the hall, his feet trudging every step with a slow heaviness.

"Thanks for all your help. I'm sure we can work this out until Claudia returns," Seth said. No matter what happened moving forward, he would be grateful for Leslie's assistance.

"You're welcome. Go tuck Toby in, and I'll take care of things in here and then head out. Goodnight, Seth."

"Goodnight." He headed down the hall and entered Toby's room. "Did you brush your teeth?"

"Yes, sir. Miss Sullivan already reminded me." *Of course she did.*

He had no reason to be upset with the pretty woman his son adored, but she made it all look so easy. *The parenting thing*. Something he himself hadn't figured out yet.

"Good job. Climb into bed and say your prayers."

When Toby finished, Seth pulled up the covers to tuck him in. "Sleep tight and don't let the bedbugs bite." It was something his grandparents always said to him, and now, he like to say it to Toby. It was another connection with the past that kept him agonizing over the guilt of not visiting them more often.

"I don't have bedbugs. Yuk," Toby said, sleepily covering a yawn.

Seth headed for the door.

"Dad?"

"Yes, Toby," Seth said, stopping to turn back.

"You were wrong about Miss Sullivan. She's not a busybody, and it doesn't sound like a nice thing to say about her."

Seth frowned. "Where did you...never mind." His son must have overheard him, and worse, repeated it to his teacher. The same woman who would now be taking care of Toby after school. Could he bungle things any worse than he kept doing? "A busybody doesn't have to be a bad thing. Like the expression, busy as a bee. That's your Miss Sullivan. She's also busy, like a bee gathering honey from flower to flower, spreading her kindness to all the children in her class."

Toby smiled. "I like that. Monday I'll make sure to tell her you do like her."

"Or not." Seth shook his head. It was his fault this conversation started, and it was time to put an end to it. "Some things shouldn't be repeated and could be taken the wrong way."

Toby yawned. "I don't understand. If you like her, why wouldn't you want her to know?"

Seth paused a moment before answering, hoping to get the words right. "Your teacher is very nice. But I don't *like* like her. It's hard to explain, so please don't say anything at all. Okay, buddy?" By the sounds of things, the warning was too late, but stopping Toby from making things worse was imperative.

"Okay, Dad. Can we go to church on Sunday? Miss Leslie told me all about the kid's church and it sounds like fun."

Seth was all too happy about the quick change in subject and was more than willing to agree, especially given it was his first real sign of interest in getting to know other kids. "Sure thing." It was a good idea and sounded like something one might read in a parenting guide. *Change negative conversation to a positive subject and something you can agree on as a diversion.*

He had gone to church as a child and loved it, but it was one of the many things that stopped after his dad left. Perhaps the reconnection would be good for both father and son. Seth returned to the kitchen and was surprised to see Leslie still there. "I thought you left?"

"I figured you had a long day, and it was the least I could do to heat up some soup and make you one of those ooey-gooey grilled cheese sandwiches."

Seth smiled. He didn't want to like the woman, but she made it difficult not to, based on her continued kindness. It was clearly not an act. But for all Seth did, trying to make things right in life with his son, it was Leslie who had swooped right in and who seemed to be taking over everything—including his son's affections.

All his life he wasn't good enough...not as a son, not as a husband, not as a partner in the law firm. And now, not as a parent. He tamped down the jealousy rising in his heart. "Thank you for being so thoughtful, when I'm sure you'd rather be home." He could be gracious when the need arose.

"It's no big deal, and I wanted to talk to you for a minute about Toby. I had hoped to see you this week, but then Claudia started picking him up and I haven't seen you."

"I thought we agreed not to go down this path and that you would let me take care of Toby, seeing as he's my son." It was a gentle reminder of the conversation they had on the first day of school.

"But he's also my student. And as his teacher, I'm concerned. Toby seems troubled and resistant to making friends. I'm just hoping that you could give me insight that might help him make the transition better."

Seth shook his head. "Thank you for caring. But he's fine, trust me. He's been through a lot of changes recently and I'm doing the best I can at the moment. It doesn't help when you start butting in and trying to psychoanalyze both of us, or worse, putting ideas in his head."

"That's not what I'm doing...I only want to help," Leslie insisted, not backing down.

"I understand that, and you can help. If you would stick to teaching him his ABC's and 123's and leave the parenting to me. Tomorrow morning, I'll try to find someone else to look after him so you don't have to go out of your way after school to help us out," he bristled. So much for working things out peacefully. They both had an agenda, but when it came to Toby, Seth was in charge of the outcome.

Leslie grimaced. "Ah yes, the busybody comment."

Seth felt a warm flush creep under his collar. Not his finest moment, not by a long shot. "I'm sorry. I didn't mean for Toby to hear me, and most certainly, didn't intend it the way it sounded to my son."

"Yes, you did, but it doesn't bother me. Not in the slightest. People can call helping one another anything they want, but in my heart, I know it's the right thing to do. It's important to me, even if you can't see or understand it," Leslie said, her voice radiating with honesty.

Seth was taken aback by her comment and rendered speechless.

"And one more thing...I don't mind staying with Toby. He's a sweet child who needs extra attention right now...through no fault of his own. Do you have a problem with that?"

He shook his head. "No." It would be like the adage about cutting off one's nose in spite of themselves, and this was certainly one of those times.

"Good. See you later. If it's any consolation, it's only two weeks. Surely you can put up with me for that long. Enjoy your dinner, Mr. Dillinger." Leslie waved and was gone before he could answer.

Prickly woman if you asked him.

Prickly sweet.

Chapter Seven

♥

It was unfortunate Claudia hadn't pre-warned Seth about the changes, but over-all, Leslie thought he had handled it well. The man worked from sunup till sundown and was trying to make things right for his son. It was the same reason she didn't understand why he wouldn't accept help when freely offered. There was nothing wrong with acts of kindness, but for whatever reason, Seth was averse to becoming the recipient. Unless it was just *her* help that he was averse to. It was a daunting thought.

Friday had gone much better at school and at home, and the beauty of it was that Toby seemed to be coming out of his shell. It wasn't anything she would point out to Seth, but it did confirm her original point. During times of change, children needed extra attention. It hadn't escaped her notice that Seth arrived back home sharply at five last night, although he claimed it was to show Toby the new horses.

Leslie wasn't so sure...as his dismissal of her was much like an echo of her own to him the previous evening. Not that she minded, since she had lots of errands to run and getting home earlier would give her a head start to get them done and make the weekend more enjoyable.

Sipping on her cup of hot coffee, Leslie savored the chicory and French vanilla flavors. She'd never been one prone to black coffee no matter how hard she tried, and the creamer added a nice touch.

Her phone pinged a notification. She glanced at the calendar on her screen and tapped on it to see what she had scheduled, not recalling anything off the top of her head.

Toby Dillinger's 7th birthday. The bright orange letters were Leslie's coded entries that she added at the beginning of each year. It was something she'd done since she started teaching, adding all the children's birthdays to make sure every child received special birthday wishes from her. To Leslie, it was the little things that counted in big ways.

Normally, she looked a few days ahead to have a forewarning, but the first week of school was always a little more hectic...and then, of course, watching Toby after school had thrown her regular schedule off kilter and she hadn't even checked her phone. Even more surprising though, was that Toby hadn't mentioned the upcoming birthday, and Seth hadn't said a thing about it either. From experience, Leslie knew kids love to talk about their birthdays, their eyes typically bright with excitement, making sure everyone around them knew it also.

Leslie pondered the situation. Weekend birthdays always made it slightly more difficult, but in a small town, it was never impossible. With all the changes going on in Toby's life, she was more concerned Seth might forget. Men were notorious for not remembering special dates...or so that was what other women had told her. A piece of their conversation floated to mind as Seth had let slip that he was taking the lead role in parenting, as if it were new to him since the divorce.

Even if he did remember, there was no way Toby's father would bake a cake. Between no cake and a store-bought cake, the imagery was more than enough to spur Leslie into action. The memory of stale store cakes, or worse, mistake cakes, as she called them, had been the norm for her childhood.

One year, her foster parents hadn't even bothered to alter the mistake name on the cake. They were more concerned about the money they saved, although she'd taken comfort that year that she had a cake at all. It was only after, when the other kids teased her that it had become a painful experience. It was only by her faith she had remained steadfast and not wavered in her graciousness, letting their taunts roll off her back. *Mostly*.

After all, even the mistake cake was better than nothing...something that had happened more times than she wanted to count. Not that there weren't wonderful foster families in this world, because there were loads of them. The problem, however, was there weren't enough. And the older Leslie got, the harder it became to place her in a new home each time. Many birthdays were spent alone at the foster home, completely forgotten.

And after all Toby had been through this year, he deserved more than that. An idea struck, one she couldn't tamp down once it started to take hold and grow. She would bake Toby a cake and drop it off at his house.

And if Seth did have something already, it would be an extra treat for Toby to have two. A twinge of guilt flitted through her brain. Was Seth right and there was a grain of truth to his busybody comment?

No. She wouldn't let him ruin her intentions and possibly Toby's birthday. Her interference was meant with a good heart and in the right spirit. *Isn't that what counted?*

Leslie made her way to the cupboard in search of the ingredients she would need and started lining them up on the counter. She tried to think of what a seven-year-old boy would like for a cake. Chocolate was all she had on hand, so chocolate it would be, but she also considered it a safe bet. What kid didn't like chocolate?

Leslie flipped through her phone and searched for ideas, pausing at the dinosaur cake. It looked easy enough. A quick check to verify she had a package of plastic dinosaurs in her decorating box revealed she was good to go.

It would take a few hours, but it was for a good cause. And maybe it had been God's plan all along that she would be free this morning to make the cake. With that knowledge firmly seated, Leslie went to work.

She mixed the batter, adding each ingredient and then stirring. The creamy batter poured out from the bowl into the oblong pan with ease, Leslie using the spatula to capture every last drop. The batter on the bottom for the cake. The batter on the sides for herself. A small indulgence when she was done with the utensil.

By the time Leslie cleaned up the kitchen, the smell of warm chocolate cake baking in the oven filled the room.

After running a load of laundry, the timer on the oven went off. Placing the pan on a cooling rack, she set out to pull this morning's load of clothes from the dryer to fold and make way for the towels.

As the cake cooled, Leslie went over the design steps, trying to visualize the finished product. With a pond and some trees, the dinosaurs would roam the forest. The edging would be the hard part, but the special tips she used to make fancy trim would make short work of the project. Folks in town enjoyed her cakes as much as she enjoyed creating them, and they brought her specialty orders quite often. Mickey Mouse, Nemo, a butterfly, and even a panda bear...you name it. She'd done so many, she lost count.

On a sheet cake, it was the frosting that brought the birthday centerpiece to life. Separating the cream cheese mixture into different bowls, she added the food coloring to tint the gooey white cream and make the proper shades needed for the design.

Using a clean knife in each bowl, one color at a time, she used delicate strokes, trying to keep the lines separate and clean. It was a slow process, but highly rewarding. Leslie was thoroughly pleased with the results and hoped Toby would appreciate them. *And perhaps even Seth.*

Her phone rang, Leslie smiling when she noticed it was her best friend. "Morning, Beth. What's up?"

"Not much. I was thinking of going to Austin to do some shopping. We haven't had an out-of-town lunch in a while. You game?"

It sounded like a lovely way to spend Saturday afternoon. "Oh, that sounds like such a good idea. Perhaps we could leave right after I deliver a birthday cake to Toby."

"Toby? You mean that hunky dad of his hired you to make a cake for his son? That's terribly sweet of him. Word gets out and that man will draw all the single ladies in town like a moth to a flame." Beth laughed.

"You are so far off base. Don't go giving credit where credit's not due. Seth did not hire me to make a cake. I didn't have a chance to tell you this yet, but Claudia had to leave town and help her sister. She asked me to watch Toby after school until she returns. So I'm taking a special interest in Toby, hoping to help his adjustment to Crossroads Creek go a little easier. I told you that from the start. Nothing more."

"I had heard about Claudia, but not about you. Talk about an inside scoop. So what, you like to hang out at the ranch now after school, waiting for your cowboy to come home?" Beth cackled. "This is rich."

"Stop. It's nothing like that and you know it. I told you before and I'll tell you again it's against the rules to date parents, and even if it wasn't a rule, I wouldn't do it. The man has no interest in me and the feelings are mutual. This is about helping Toby and I would never do anything that could hurt the child. End of story," Leslie declared. Perhaps a little overboard, but better to set the record straight.

"*Bah humbug*. I think you protest too much," Beth said.

Leslie shook her head, knowing her friend was an endless romantic...for everyone but herself at the moment. Two could play her game. "Quit pushing the cowboy on me. If you think he's so hunky, he's all yours."

"And you know that's not going to happen. Not a chance. After Jerry, I'm lying low for a while. So do you want to meet around eleven?"

she asked, apparently more than ready for a change in conversation.

"That sounds great." Leslie hung up the phone, and then carefully boxed up the cake. Placing it on the front seat of the car, she put cushions around the carton to hold it in place, being extra careful not to press against the top and mess up the frosting. After running back in the house for a box of candles, she slid into the car and headed for the Dillinger ranch.

Seth's truck was parked out front, which meant she was in luck and they were home. It wouldn't take long to drop off the cake and wish Toby a happy birthday. She couldn't wait to see his eyes light up with joy.

Leslie stepped up onto the front porch and pulled open the screen door, propping it open with her foot. Carefully balancing the cake box in one arm, she raised her hand to knock just as the door opened. "Hi—"

Seth slammed into her as he barreled through the door, knocking the cake from her hand. Leslie watched in horror as it smashed to the porch, the plastic wrap coming loose as chunks of cake, dinosaurs, and colored frosting flew everywhere, spattering the rails, some even landing on her shoe.

"What the—"

"*Noooo*," Leslie wailed. "Look at what you've done." All of her hard work, ruined in a split second. Toby's surprise was officially a disaster.

"Me? I was just coming out of the house. What are you doing here and what is that?" he asked, grimacing as he pointed at the mess.

"A cake. Or it was," she added. A movement behind Seth caught her attention. *Toby*.

He glanced down at the heaping pile of mush and then up at her.

"Happy birthday, Toby. I'm so sorry about your cake. I wanted to surprise you." She was trying to keep it all together for the child's sake.

"Thank you," he mumbled, his lower lip quivering ever so slightly but just enough that

Leslie noticed, as well as picking up on the tears that glistened in his eyes.

"A birthday cake? You don't say." Seth stood there shaking his head. His expression, one of guilt, couldn't be mistaken for anything else.

He had forgotten. Making the cake disaster even worse if that were possible.

Seth clapped his son on the shoulder. "Yes, happy birthday, Toby. With everything going on this morning, I'd plumb forgotten."

It was a good recovery, but Leslie knew the truth.

"It's okay," Toby mumbled. "My cake's not, but I'm sure you have something planned for me later. Maybe Miss Sullivan can celebrate with us. It's not like I have any friends coming over."

And therein lay his lack of excitement. Leslie felt honored by his request but would let Seth off the hook this time. "I've got some plans this afternoon and then I want to go home and make you another cake, young man. I'm sure your father has a special birthday planned for you, and I wouldn't want to interfere."

Seth cleared his throat. "Not so fast, Leslie. I mean, *ummm*, Toby's got a point. Can I talk to you privately for a minute?"

It was an odd request, and for curiosity's sake alone, she would agree. "Sure." They stepped off the porch.

"We'll be right back, Toby. It's about your birthday so we can't have you listening in," Seth said, smiling at his son.

"What's going on?" Leslie asked.

"First, I'm sorry about the cake. I was in a rush and not paying attention."

His apology was genuine, and it took the knee-jerk sting out of the disaster. "Thank you. You do a lot of rushing around. Perhaps you should slow down a bit for Toby's sake," she added gently.

Seth nodded. "Point taken. And on that note, I'm hoping we can put aside our different opinions temporarily. For Toby's sake, that is. I need your help to make this day special, and I'm hoping you can't resist saying yes. For Toby's sake," he added, making sure they were on the same page by reiterating her comment.

"What kind of help?" she asked, intrigued by the sudden change in Seth.

"I'm sure you've realized by now that I forgot his birthday. It was always Alicia who took care of events like this. It's no excuse, and what's done is done. But I am hoping to get better at these kinds of things, which is where you come in. I need to shop for his birthday presents, and I need to buy a cake since there's no way I can ask you to make another one. But I've got to check in on the mares and pick up some vitamins at the vets," Seth said, desperation in his voice. "

All the more reason for Leslie to continue to make this easy on him. Something she had the power to do. "You don't have to ask, I'm offering. I grew up on store-bought cakes and they aren't anything like homemade. The dinosaurs bit the dust, but I'll figure something else out."

Seth nodded. "Thank you so much. Every little bit helps."

"Maybe if we go into town together, you can get what you need at the vets and get Toby's gifts, while I shop for the groceries."

"That sounds even better. So much of our future is riding on these two mares, I've got to do everything just right."

The cowboy didn't know it yet, but Leslie had an agenda. "Only if you agree to make the cake with me. You need to get more involved, not just be a bystander in Toby's life. This might be the best birthday gift you could give him. The future is now. Fit the mares in your schedule...not Toby." It was a big push, but Seth needed to step up to the plate and handle his new parenting role.

Seth seemed taken aback at her forthright comment. "You drive a hard bargain. And be forewarned, I don't cook."

Leslie grinned. "I'll be right there with you to make sure all goes well. I promise."

"Okay, then. Just don't make me wear an apron or a hat," he teased, his rare smile lighting his face and softening his features.

It would seem Seth *did* know how to have fun. The trick was getting him to do it more often.

Chapter Eight

♥

SETH COULDN'T BELIEVE HE had forgotten Toby's birthday. And if not for Leslie, he would have let the day slip by unnoticed, putting him solidly in the not-good-at-parenting category. It seemed the harder he tried, the worse he did. Leslie's generosity had saved the day. Period. How could he be upset with a woman whose generosity and heart had a mind of her own, and his son was the beneficiary?

"Toby," Seth said, returning to the porch, "we've decided to run into town and Miss Sullivan is going to pick up the ingredients to make a cake, while I tend to some other things. Then we can all come back here and you can watch the adults make a new cake. What do you say to those plans?"

Toby's face lit up, his answer obvious even before his son spoke. "You mean it? You're going to bake a cake. This I've got to see."

"And Miss Sullivan, as I'm sure you don't want me to make it by myself. Not if you want to actually eat the cake," he added, shooting a grin at Leslie.

Leslie shook her head. "I don't want to ask the obvious about your lack of cooking abilities, but I find I must. If you can't cook...what were you two eating before I showed up and started fixing your dinner?"

"Simple stuff." Seth shrugged. Simple as in it came out of a box or a can. *Who had time for anything else?* It's not like they were going hungry, not by a long shot.

"I see," Leslie said, her voice tinged with doubt. "I'm ready if you all are."

They slid into the truck, Toby choosing to ride up front between them. Conversation flowed freely, but then Toby's excitement as he tried to decide on one cake design made it easy.

"Okay, I know what I want. For sure, this time," Toby added. "A firetruck. I'm getting too old for dinosaurs."

Seth frowned, nudging Toby with his elbow, hoping to send a clear message without words. It only took a second.

"Sorry, Miss Sullivan. I'm sure the dinosaur cake was cool. It's just that I want to be a fireman when I grow up and I think a red firetruck cake would be awesome."

Leslie grinned at Toby. "It's not a problem, and I totally understand. You are getting older and it makes perfect sense. Why do you want to be a fireman?"

"My best friend's dad is a fireman. We got to do fun stuff with him down at the fire station. And we got to ride on the truck, and blow the horn, and even wear a fireman's hat," Toby said, his voice animated.

"Sounds like you had quite a lot of adventure. Perhaps one day I should take you to the volunteer fire department here in Crossroads Creek and introduce you to the firemen," Leslie said.

Seth had heard it all before from Toby, only this time, the comments seemed to rub him the wrong way. When he was busy at the law office, none of this bothered him. And a career in law didn't seem like such a good choice, given all that had happened. Starting over on the ground floor at a new office was never a choice for Seth. Not to mention, few kids grew up wanting to be a corporate attorney as most considered it boring. Although on the upside, it helped Seth immensely when it came to negotiating contracts on the new horses.

Now, however, it would be totally cool if his son wanted to be just like him...a horse breeder. Someone to work the ranch for him and take over when the time was right. After all, wasn't that why he wanted to restore the ranch? A home for them, yes, but the legacy for his son. If he could make it all work. There was so much riding on the mares testing positive as pregnant. Patience was normally needed as it took three to four months to find out via ultrasound. Months Seth didn't have, which is why he had arranged for a vet from Dallas with expertise in the field to come in and check for earlier results.

Seth smiled at Toby, giving him a nod of approval for sidestepping the slightly rude comment, so as not to offend Leslie. Pulling up to the front door area of the Super Saver grocery store, he glanced at his watch. "I'll see you in about forty-five minutes. If you think that will work, that is."

"More than enough time, but there are a few extra things on my agenda I'd like to take care of."

Given he still considered the woman a busybody, it made him think twice about what she was up to. "Do I want to ask?"

Leslie shook her head and grinned. "No. Trust me on this one."

"I don't see as I have much choice considering all you've done and are doing for Toby today."

The pair slid out of the truck and disappeared into the store, waving before the door closed behind them. Seth drove to Haskins Five & Dime, having noticed a toy section in the back corner on several of his earlier visits. It wasn't overflowing with the latest toys in every size, shape, and color, but he figured the choice would be plentiful enough to find a few gifts for Toby.

He stopped to read the poster on the front window, the cutest picture of a puppy catching his attention. It would go a long way to making Toby happy, but Seth just couldn't do it. Not yet. Maybe when things settled down, but it would be a mistake now.

Greg Haskins greeted him at the door. "Good morning. What can I do for you, Seth? Need some more supplies for the ranch?"

The man moved slowly, as he was a bit on the portly side and elderly. What hair he had was thin and gray and gelled into place. But when it came to his store, he was on top of things and sharp as a tack. The store was like a one-stop shop for clothes, toys, household supplies, and it served as the town's hardware store.

"No supplies today. It's my son's birthday and I need some presents. Any idea what to get a seven-year-old?" he asked, not up on what's hot and what's not in a child's world.

"Follow me...I've got just the ticket to make your present a hit."

Seth followed, his gaze landing on the bike rack as they passed by it. When they left L.A., he had paired down everything they owned, not seeing much use for the fancy home furnishings. Toby's bike was one of the things left behind since he had outgrown it.

"Here we are, the newest fire truck on the market, with all the bells and whistles." Greg picked up the box and handed it to Seth. "It's got more moving parts than a real fire truck." He chuckled.

The man's exaggeration got the message across quite nicely, but seriously...a firetruck? It was as though the world was conspiring against him. They were already making a firetruck cake, so this was a gift he wouldn't mind skipping. "I think not."

Greg arched an eyebrow up as he nodded, an odd, questioning look on his face. "Well, then...let me see. What about this action hero super costume pack? Most children love to be action heroes and with Halloween next month, it could serve double duty. He could wear it to the Bobbing for Apples party at the church, a local favorite for kids around here."

Seth hadn't known about the party and he stored the information away for later. "I don't know. The truth is, I don't know what Toby likes." *Besides firetrucks and puppies.* Neither of which he wanted to get for his son as a birthday present.

Moving forward, Seth figured it was an area that deserved more attention. It was so hard to know all the aspects of good parenting and so far, he hadn't done so great.

"My grandson plays games on his tablet a lot. There are tons of educational games you can add that make learning fun, and they don't even realize you have an agenda," Greg offered.

Seth nodded. "That sounds good. I'll take one of those."

He moved to the checkout line, standing behind another customer. The mother and son laughed and joked. The kid was all too happy he was about to own a skateboard. And a helmet. And safety pads. And a jacket. But it was the last item she pulled out of her cart that grabbed Seth's attention the most. *A firetruck.*

He groaned, looking down at the single object in his hand. The woman finished up with her purchase and was soon on her way out of the store.

Greg rang up the tablet. "Your total is $129 .74," he said, sliding the gift into a bag.

Glancing at the door and then back at his purchase, the urge to do more flared. A kid only had one seventh birthday, and this was Seth's first-time handling the responsibility for it. Something he almost messed up. "On second thought, can you add the firetruck? And a skateboard, the helmet, and the pads, just like the ones the lady before me bought. Oh, and add the red bike over there," he said, pointing to the bike rack. If the firetruck would make Toby happy, that's all that mattered.

Greg Haskins grinned an all-knowing smile. "Sure thing. I've got the prices right here from her ticket, and I know the price of the bike. We can gather up the rest of your order after we ring it out. Will that be all then?"

Seth nodded. "Yes."

"Are you sure?" Greg asked, a teasing smile on his face.

"I'm sure." Seth had the question coming given that he'd come to the line with one item and just bought six things. He pulled out his credit card to pay for the order. It had been an impulsive decision, but Seth was sure it would make him father-of-the-year in Toby's eyes, and he couldn't wait to see his son's reaction.

He finished paying for everything. "Do you think you could deliver all this a little later today? I want to surprise Toby and I've only got the truck, and he's with me. Kind of hard to hide a bike." Seth grinned.

"Sure thing. There's a ten-dollar local delivery charge, if that's all right with you," Greg asked.

"Of course. Thank you. And here's an extra twenty dollars if you wrap the gifts," Seth offered, holding out another bill.

Greg shook his head. "Sorry, but that's where I draw the line and the missus isn't home at the moment. Trust me, you don't want me wrapping anything. The drugstore next door has cards, wrapping paper, and tape if you need them."

"Good enough." Stuffing the money back in his front pocket, Seth waved farewell and then made his way to the drugstore. Once inside, he found everything he needed to gift wrap the presents after they were delivered, but he also spotted party decorations.

And it was a birthday party.

There were several options but giving in once again to what Toby might choose, Seth settled on the firetruck plates and napkins, even going all in and getting the red plastic silverware. Adding signs to hang up, a few table covers, and even some matching cups, he picked out everything they offered in the fireman line.

This would be a real party of three...that is, if he could convince Leslie to stay.

With three minutes to spare, he pulled up to the Super Saver and waited for Leslie and Toby to appear. He didn't have to wait long. They had an awful lot of groceries for one cake, the cart overflowing with bags. Seth planned to reimburse Leslie for the expenses...make that double the reimbursement, considering he had ruined the first cake.

Seth waited by the truck. "How did it go?" he asked as they approached. He grabbed two of the bags and loaded them into the bed, securing them in the corner.

"Fabulous, and then some," Leslie said, a huge smile on her face that reached her eyes. "Toby, why don't you get buckled in while we take care of the groceries?"

It reminded him of Leslie's earlier comment about trusting her. It would seem he was about to find out exactly what she was up to.

"Sure thing, Miss Sullivan. After all, it's my birthday so I don't have to do any work. Not even clean my room. Right, Dad?" Toby asked, a hopeful expression on his face.

"Sure thing, buddy."

Leslie grabbed a few of the bags and handed them to Seth. "I actually needed to talk to you. Alone," she said in a hushed voice.

It was nothing more than he figured. "What's up?" He paused what he was doing to give her his full attention.

"I'm hoping you won't get upset, but I had the best idea ever and I acted on it. I'm sort of impulsive like that," Leslie teased.

Seth agreed but kept that part to himself. "Let's hear your idea."

"A surprise birthday party for Toby," she said, glancing toward the cab of the truck to make sure the birthday boy wasn't listening.

"Oh, is that all? I'm so glad you asked. It works for me because I was trying to figure out how to convince you to join us for dinner and a celebration tonight. Three people can be a party in my books." And if he was lucky, perhaps Leslie would do the wrapping. His own wrapping skills he felt sure would be worse than old man Haskins given his lack of experience.

Leslie winced. "*Ummm*, not quite. More like eighteen at last count."

"I'm not following you."

"Here's the deal. I called Beth to cancel our plans for this afternoon, so we're no longer going to Austin. When I told her why, we got to brainstorming and she agreed to help us throw a surprise party. I sent her a text with a class listing of students contact information. So far, seven kids are coming, each with a parent. Add Beth, me, you, and Toby and that makes eighteen."

Eighteen people. At his house. Tonight. *Was she out of her mind?* "An actual full-blown party. I've never hosted a get together, much less a kid's birthday party and wouldn't know the first thing about it. You should have talked to me first." Not to mention even if he did know these things, it's not like there would be enough time to put it all together.

"You don't know what it takes, but I do. And so does Beth. I've got it all under control as long as you don't say no," Leslie said, a hopeful expression on her face.

Seth shook his head but knew there was only one answer he could give. "Doesn't sound like I have much choice, seeing as everyone is planning to show up anyway."

Her smile faded. "True. But you could be happier about it," Leslie urged.

Seth let out a deep breath. "If it makes Toby happy, it's all good. It's his special day and who am I to stand in the way of his happiness?" Isn't that the same reason he went overboard buying gifts?

"Thank you. You won't regret it, I promise. Working together, I'm sure we can pull this off.

I'm hoping Toby will make more friends this way. I thought of it as a win/win situation."

Her reasoning was solid, even if she might have overstepped her boundaries yet again. "It would seem you think of everything, Miss Sullivan."

"Not everything. I forgot to go back and pick up extra burgers and buns when more people texted they could come to the party. I've got to run back into the store for the rest."

"Would pizza be okay?" he offered. "I make a killer frozen pizza."

Leslie grinned. "Killer frozen pizza? I'm not sure anyone can pull that off. But I'm guessing if you have at least five or six of them, it would work."

"I do and it is. Killer, that is. You haven't had pizza till you've had mine," Seth boasted. But then it was one of Toby's favorite meals since they'd moved to Crossroads Creek. That and blue box Macaroni and Cheese.

"I almost hate to ask, but what do you do with the pizza?"

"Doctor it," he added matter-of-factly, walking away to push the cart back into one of the corrals.

Leslie might have been a little high-handed in planning a party on such a grand scale, but it would leave him looking even more like a hero dad. Except he didn't deserve credit for the party. It was all Leslie's doing and he wouldn't take credit.

Seth returned to the truck where Leslie waited. "So why aren't you married and a passel of kids of your own? You seem to have the motherly instincts down pat," he teased.

Her expression darkened. "My students are my children. Why do I need more? And as to instinct...I simply try to do what's in a child's best interests." With that, she rounded the truck and slid inside without so much as a backward glance.

Her response baffled him. He'd meant the comment as a compliment, so why Leslie was upset, he couldn't begin to fathom. That's what he got for trying to be nice.

Chapter Nine

♥

LESLIE COULDN'T STOP THE ache Seth's comment started deep within her heart. Not that he'd done it intentionally, as clearly he didn't know her situation. No one except Beth and her doctor knew for that matter, and of course...Brad. The man she thought she would marry, but who broke her heart instead when he found out about her medical condition. Some women didn't want children, others got married and had kids. And then there were women like her...women who wanted children but couldn't have them. Which wouldn't have been so much of an issue if society didn't feel children should be raised by two parents. Less than one percent of adoptions went to single parents, and as a teacher, she couldn't even begin to afford the expense. Instead, she'd learned to trust in God a long time ago and had learned to live with the medical condition that prevented her from having children.

It was also one of the reasons she had gone into the education field. To make a difference in children's lives, even if they weren't her own. She tried to shake off the melancholy that had settled in.

Seth parked the truck in front of the house and they worked together to unload the food. Toby had been excused from helping, allowing him the luxury to enjoy his birthday.

Once in the kitchen, by the time she had laid out all the ingredients, Toby had magically appeared. The irony of having both the Dillinger men as students made her smile. The two of them sat on the stools, bellied up to the counter, ready to watch. She knew Seth had hoped that the working together part would mostly land on Leslie's shoulders, but she had a different style of teaching. *Hands on.*

Leslie's gaze landed on Seth. "You know, helping me make this cake does not involve sitting on that stool watching. Only Toby gets those honors," she chided.

"Yeah, Dad. I want to see you make a cake. That's something I've never seen before," Toby agreed, grinning up at his father.

Seth shook his head. "Can't blame me for trying, but it doesn't look like I have much chance of getting out of this. Two against one, I reckon I should give in graciously. But don't say I didn't warn you...this might not be an edible cake when I'm done with it. Not to mention, it most likely won't even resemble a fire truck." He looked at them, a hopeful expression on his face, but neither Toby nor Leslie would budge on this one.

"That's what I'm here for. It'll be just fine," Leslie said, shooting a grin at Seth, hoping to reassure him.

The corners of his eyes crinkled when he smiled, his eyes lit with laughter. It was difficult to stay focused when he relaxed. Leslie forced herself to remember he was simply another student at the moment. Professionalism was in order. Although, a much older student by way of a man, and unfortunately, one that sent her heart racing with his handsome good looks and current easy demeanor.

"Step one. Dump both these packages of mix into the bowl. We are doubling the recipe to make sure we can make a bigger cake. If you read the recipe on the back of the box, it tells you exactly what to do. Fool proof, honestly. And I have it on good authority you can read, so no excuses," she teased.

"Smart aleck." Seth cut open the bag and emptied the contents into the bowl.

Leslie held out the box and pointed at the instructions. "Step two. Preheat the oven. The temperature is listed right here." She tapped at the bottom of the recipe.

"Are you teaching or helping?" Seth asked.

"Teaching. This is a seriously needed skill set for a single dad." Leslie shot him a playful smile, enjoying the camaraderie. "Keep reading."

"Fine."

Step by step, he called out the directions and step by step, Leslie handed him what he needed. Measuring cups. Oil. Water. Blender. Spatula. From teacher to sous chef. Both labels worked.

"Add three eggs and blend," Seth said, holding out his hand.

"You mean six, right? Because of the doubling." Leslie handed him the first egg.

"Yes, that's what I meant."

"Sure you did," she teased. "You have cracked an egg before, haven't you?"

Seth nodded. "Of course. I do cook breakfast on occasion," he added when he noted her expression of disbelief.

"I wasn't sure. Just remember, the most important thing is not to get the shells in the batter. We don't care if they break because we're going to blend them anyway. Just give it one sharp crack on the side. Then, using your thumbs, gently pull the shell apart, letting the egg drop into the bowl. It's safer to crack them into a different bowl in case you have to get out a piece of shell or to make sure that there's nothing wrong with the egg. We wouldn't want to lose everything from one bad egg now, would we?" Leslie smiled, giving him the extra tips and tricks of cracking an egg whether he wanted to hear them or not.

"A bad egg would be totally yucky in my cake," Toby chimed in, his nose scrunched up in distaste.

Leslie laughed. "That's for sure. And I'm glad we're all in agreement. No bad eggs allowed."

Seth finished breaking the eggs open and looked up at her, holding the bowl out for her inspection.

"Good work."

"I told you I was a master at egg breaking," he said, his eyes twinkling with mirth.

This was the most relaxed she had ever seen Seth. So it's not whether he knew how, but more a case of if he chose to exercise the casual way. Perhaps along the way of helping Toby, she might be helping his father adjust as well. She wouldn't be doing it for any personal reason of her own, other than kindness. There was clearly a very special reason God had brought them into her life, and she would do her best to help them both move forward with theirs.

Seth read the next direction and Leslie held out the mixer after inserting the two wire beaters. "Make sure you —"

The mixer roared to life, splattering chocolate and egg everywhere.

"Stoppp," Leslie shrieked, jumping back, and reaching for the power cord to shut the appliance off. "Master egg breaker, rotten mixer," she said, latching on to a towel next to the sink to wipe the splatters off her shirt and face.

"Sorry," Seth said, unable to hide his laughter.

Toby joined in, the two having fun at her expense.

"How is it you managed to get none on you and all of it on me? If I didn't know any better,

I'd think you planned it," she said, unable to stop from joining in the fun. It was only batter...and chocolate at that. Her favorite.

Toby reached out and used his finger to swipe at a few splotches that had landed on the counter. "*Hmmm*, I love chocolate."

"Something we have in common. And since it's your birthday, I may even let you scrape the leftovers when we're done, if your dad manages to keep some of it in the bowl," she teased.

"That sounds yummy. I've never done that before," Toby said.

"You're kidding? That's always the best part."

Seth reached out, his hand moving toward her as though in slow motion. He took the towel from her and wiped it gently across her forehead and then down her hair. "You missed a few spots," he said, chuckling.

"Thanks. You're forgiven. At least you didn't let me go the rest of the afternoon with chocolate on my face."

His grin widened. "I was tempted, but I figured Toby would rat me out."

Leslie picked up the baking pan to prepare and grease it with butter. It was the least she could do to help, knowing it was the messiest part of making a cake. *That is, unless Seth Dillinger was mixing the batter.* "Try it again. This time, start slow and occasionally use the spatula to move it off the outer edges and into the center so it all comes out nice and evenly blended."

"Yes, boss." Seth shot her a grin.

"I like the sound of that. But then, you get to do all this work now, because I plan to decorate the cake. That's the teamwork part of it. Judging by your mixing skills, I'm pretty sure I should trust you when you say you would make a mess of the decorating. Perhaps some other time we can practice that skill, but not today. Not on Toby's birthday."

"Dad doesn't know how to decorate because he was always busy at the office and my mom had to do it. She didn't like making me a cake either."

"I'm sorry, Toby," Seth said, suddenly serious.

The light-hearted tone in the kitchen dwindled.

"It's okay. I am good at decorating and enjoy it every minute," she said, coming to the rescue.

"Maybe I can help you," Toby offered, his earlier comment forgotten.

Leslie nodded. "That sounds like a grand idea."

It wasn't long before the cake was in the oven and the warm smell of baking chocolate filled the kitchen air and permeated through the whole house. They had decided the weather was perfect for an outdoor party and Beth was due to arrive any time to help them start setting up.

Seth brought out several folding tables, along with a couple of coolers for drinks.

Beth pulled up and parked her car.

Leslie hugged her friend. "I'm so glad you agreed to help us. And we'll definitely plan another day in Austin, I promise."

"No worries. Besides, this sounds like way more fun," Beth said, smirking.

"A seven-year-old's birthday party?" Leslie asked with a slight shake of her head.

Beth put an arm around her shoulder as the two of them headed back to where Seth and Toby waited. "No, watching you and the cowboy."

Leslie stopped short. "Don't start, Beth. You know the rules as well as I do."

"There's nothing in the school rules about looking."

Enough was enough. "Then have at it, because you get to finish setting up out here, and I'll be inside working on the cake. Our guests are due to arrive in about an hour, so we don't have much time. Were you able to get the extra party supplies at the drugstore?"

"You asked, and I delivered," Beth said holding up a giant bag of supplies.

"Perfect. And you can put Toby's present on the table over there," Leslie added, as she pointed to where several gifts had been placed. Mr. Haskins had personally delivered the gifts...already wrapped, of all things.

"Don't be such a fuddy duddy. Loosen up and have some fun." Beth was forever hounding her to date, but they both knew dating led to a serious relationship. And a serious relationship could lead to commitment. And therefore, the need to confide in someone with her problem. And she wasn't willing to risk the disappointment in another man's eyes.

Leslie walked away toward the house, finding it easier to ignore the comment. It took her the better part of two hours to decorate the cake, especially with everyone coming in and out of the kitchen to check on her progress. The Oreo cookie wheels had been easy enough, as was the licorice hose wound up on the side. It was the double-decker cake with red frosting and white trim that proved the most difficult. Of course, the gum drop lights added just the right touch and luckily were easy enough to add.

Toby had forgotten his offer to help, but it was all for the good, as she needed to focus on the details. Until the cake was done, no one got to see her newest creation. To her, it was like the unveiling of a masterpiece.

She stepped back to see her design. The fire truck turned out even better than the dinosaur cake and had certainly been more fun to make.

Leslie could hear voices from outside and she glanced out the front living room window, excited to see the first of the guests arriving. Toby was in his element as he greeted Ava, his only school friend at the moment. Something Leslie hoped to change today. She dropped the drape back into place, smiling. She picked up the cake and made her way to the front door, saying a little prayer for the safety of her treasured cargo. After verifying Seth was nowhere around, she pushed open the screen door with her foot and made her way down the steps and to the food table.

Beth was the first to join her. "Wow. That looks fabulous, Leslie. I hope you charged Seth double since you had to make two cakes."

Leslie shook her head. "I'm not charging him at all. This is my gift to Toby."

"You're such a softie. Face it, you're interested, whether you admit it or not."

Leslie tried to think of a quick retort, but none would come.

Toby came running up with Ava to see the cake. His mouth dropped wide open. "That's my cake? Wow. This is the coolest cake ever."

Leslie felt a rush of relief surge through her body. This was always the most important moment...knowing if the recipient loved the cake design as much as she did. "I'm so glad you like it."

"Like it? I love it." Toby beamed.

The inspiration to make a double-decker firetruck cake to give it a more 3D effect had occurred to her as she was getting ready to start the decorating process. Simply making the truck shorter gave her the extra sections she needed to go higher. It was a bit crumbly when it came to frosting, but with patience, it all worked out perfectly.

Seth came over with a couple of the newcomers who had just arrived. Angela was a single mother and hung on to Seth's arms as if whatever he'd been saying had been the most important thing in the world.

Not that Leslie cared or was paying close attention.

Seth stepped in close. "Wow, the cake looks great. Maybe you can make my birthday cake," he said, paying her the best compliment possible.

Repeat business.

"Leslie makes cakes for a lot of people in town. She's the best," Angela said, batting her long eyelashes at the cowboy.

"You can say that again. At least when it comes to saving the day and making cakes." He added, shooting Leslie a wink.

Angela frowned, glancing back and forth between Seth and Leslie.

Let her think what she wanted, because if she was connecting Seth and her together, she'd be wrong. "Why thank you. I do believe that's a very nice compliment," Leslie said, pulling out all stops to be equally pleasant.

Seth smiled. "We don't always see eye to eye, but we do today, and that's what counts."

Of course, it was only for today.

Seth was doing this for Toby. The kindness act was for the benefit of his son. Seth Dillinger was no closer to learning how to interact with others or her than he was before she arrived this morning. Even Angela hadn't been able to put a dent in the wall surrounding Seth. What would it take to get through to him to see that a small town was all about community and kindness?

Leslie pushed the thought aside, intent on enjoying the activities and games as some of the other kids from Toby's class arrived with their parents.

The weekend was over all too quickly for Seth, but it had certainly been action packed.

He had enjoyed himself at Toby's birthday party far more than he expected, thanks to Leslie. The energy that woman gave into everything she did was remarkable. Her can-do attitude had not only managed two birthday cakes, but she had pulled off a birthday party Toby wouldn't soon forget. It was encouraging to see his son laugh and play with some of the other children. At first, it was as though the kids had divided up into groups like at school, and Toby wasn't a part of any of them. It was Leslie to the rescue, with a limitless list of games to entertain the group as a whole.

Moving forward, Seth would be more than a little surprised if his son asked to stay home again. With a new circle of friends, the school would hold much greater appeal than working with him on the ranch.

He hadn't even minded meeting some of the folks from town. Even Angela and her obvious interest, even though he'd given her no reason to feel the interest was reciprocated. It was the folks who felt inclined to offer up suggestions on how to raise his son as a single father, which rubbed him the wrong way. They meant well, but Toby was his son and there was no way he would rely on their outpouring of *friendly advice*. Seth had been down that road before and been burned. Repeatedly. His father. His wife. His career.

Moving back to Crossroads Creek, he was on his own, and this time, he would be in control of his life...without interference. This was his shot to get things right with Toby and prove he could be a good father. Something he hadn't been doing while at the office. And something his father hadn't done with him—but something Seth vowed to change.

And then there was today. Toby's request to go to church had been met with approval earlier in the week, but what Seth hadn't expected was to find out why Toby was so determined to go to Sunday school. This morning, the answer was obvious. *Leslie Sullivan.*

The pretty lady kept her time card filled, it would seem. First grade elementary school teacher, Sunday school teacher, cake designer, local volunteer. No wonder everyone in town thought of her as a paragon.

The problem was...everyone included his son. Toby was enamored of the woman, but then, her motherly ways were hard not to like. Seth needed to find a way to set Toby straight. It wouldn't do any good for his son to start getting ideas about the two of them, and after yesterday, it was a possibility.

Except Seth wanted nothing more than a single-parent relationship focused on raising his son right and to get the Dillinger Horse Ranch successfully back in business. There wasn't the time or desire for anything else. Especially not Toby's temporary, beautiful nanny.

Even the message this morning at church had hit Seth hard. It was as though he was being tackled from all sides, which only served to make him dig his heels in harder. Pastor Phil was clear in his message—God was in control.

But if that was true, then why was Toby motherless, and why did Seth have a failed marriage and no career to show for the last ten years of his life?

The problem was...everything was his own fault and he couldn't blame God. The desire for the prestigious title of partner had driven every move they made, but it wasn't a good reason to get married and start a family. They had created the perfect, albeit artificial front, but in the end, it failed. Miserably. The divorce, however, was on Alicia, as Seth would have stuck it out for Toby's sake.

At least for this weekend, his son had been happy.

All thanks to Leslie, Seth had gotten it right.

Chapter Ten

♥

THE STRONG ODOR OF manure, horse, and hay greeted Leslie and Toby as they entered the barn.

"I know there's a rake in the supply shed. I saw it," Toby said. Except somehow, his destination ended at the stalls where Genevieve and Lady Jane were stalled.

"I think you wanted to come see the horses, not rake leaves," Leslie said, calling Toby out for the ruse.

"These horses are really big, aren't they?" He reached out to touch Genevieve's nose, the mare sniffing the newcomer to the barn.

She noticed he hadn't confirmed or denied her comment, but it was somewhat rhetorical anyway. His interest in horses didn't come as a surprise. Like father, like son. The horse seemed friendly enough, which was good. "They are at that. Not to mention, regal." Leslie followed Toby's lead and rubbed Lady Jane's nose, not wanting the other mare to feel left out. "We probably shouldn't bother them. The vet was just here and I know your dad said he's hoping they're pregnant. We wouldn't want to do anything to upset them."

"Will he keep the babies?" Toby asked.

"Foals. They're called foals. And I'm not sure. Maybe he'll sell some and keep others. I know he wants to have lots of horses, but I don't know much about breeding horses." Seth never said much about the business, however, she knew he was stressed about it all the time. She also understood he had a lot riding on the mares and the success of the ranch, but it wasn't healthy. Not the way he kept pushing himself and the hours he worked. Something had to give.

"Goodie. Maybe then I can finally ride one. I would love a little pony."

"Come on, let's go find the rake," Leslie said, taking Toby by the hand to head for the tool shed at the back.

They searched and searched but it was nowhere to be found. "That stinks. I really wanted to jump in the leaves."

So maybe it had been both the horses and the rake that drew Toby to the barn. "Hang on, there's one last place I can think of to look. The loft." She climbed the ladder, just far enough to peek over the edge. There wasn't a rake anywhere in sight, but her gaze landed on a rope hanging from the rafters and tied off to a beam at the side. And on the other side of the loft...a huge pile of old hay.

"Toby, you've got to see this," Leslie said, lowering herself down the ladder.

"What is it?" he asked, suddenly curious.

"A rope swing by the look of things. It doesn't look like it's been used in a while. Maybe your dad even used to swing on it. How cool would that be?"

Toby's eyes widened. "Totally cool. Let me see," he said, starting up the ladder without so much as a second thought.

"Be careful. I'll be right behind you," Leslie said, making sure he didn't slip. After Toby hauled himself upright, Leslie followed suit, dusting off her jeans. *Ha-choo.* The dust was a bit much, but Toby didn't seem to be affected. *Ha-choo.* "I probably can't stay up here long, but let's test this out," she offered, energized by the find. She'd never played on a rope swing, so for Leslie, this would be a real treat. Certainly one she didn't want to miss.

Untying the rope, she handed it to Toby. "Careful now," she said when he moved to climb up the bales stacked up as a launch pad. "Use your feet on the low knot to hold yourself up, and when you get to the pile of hay...let go."

"Wheee," he squealed, flying past her like Tarzan, the happy smile on his face making it all worth it. He landed easily, rolled over, and stood. "That was awesome. Your turn, Miss Sullivan."

Leslie checked that her phone was securely in her front pocket, not wanting to crack her screen on the landing. She wasn't sure if it would break the phone, or bruise her backside, but neither choice was appealing. Approaching the rope, she pulled herself up onto the small platform. "Here I go," she said, laughing like a little kid. Pushing off, she felt as though she were flying. "Woohoo." She landed with a thud on the pile of hay. Not that it hurt, but clearly her size and weight was a detriment compared to that of a young boy. She stood and turned back to see Toby already grabbing the rope and moving into place.

"Wasn't that awesome? It's my turn again," he said, climbing onto the platform. "I wonder if my dad will come and play with me out here?"

Leslie nodded, but as to the answer to the question, she had her reservations. "I'm sure he will. He might have forgotten all about it since he hasn't been here in such a long time." There was nothing wrong with giving the kid hope.

"I can't wait to show him." Toby beamed.

Leslie would prefer not to go again, at least not until the landing pile was padded a little more. Toby sailed through the air with ease, showing off a little this time around, as he held on with one arm and waved.

"Your turn," he said, handing her the rope just as her phone rang.

Saved by the bell...literally. "You go again. I need to take this call from Mrs. Mitchell."

Toby didn't need to be told twice, the kid off and climbing for a repeat flight.

Leslie clicked the answer button. "Hello, Claudia."

"Good afternoon, dearie," the older woman said, her voice bright.

She was a paragon of positive attitude, her glass always half full. It was one of the many reasons Leslie adored her. "You're timing is impeccable," Leslie said, lowering her voice a bit as she kept an eye on Toby.

"Why is that?" Claudia asked.

"I'm in the barn with Toby and we found an old rope swing in the loft. Toby is having a blast, me, not so much. I tried it, but once was enough."

"I remember that swing. Seth played up there all the time until he was about Toby's age. Lloyd Dillinger, Seth's grandfather, hung that swing for his son, Robert. And then, after the fallout between Robert and Janice, Robert left town. Grace and Lloyd never got over their son running out on his family, and they never forgave Robert or Janice. It was only when Seth's mother visited the ranch that he got to play after that. He was such a serious young man, but occasionally, he knew how to have fun."

Claudia prattled on, but the information was enlightening and Leslie could no more stop her from telling the story than she could stop breathing. It explained so much about Seth and what he must have gone through...and was going through again with the divorce and single parenting. Her respect climbed another notch or two, knowing how hard it was to fight back against what was happening when you were just a child caught up in what should have been a trusted adult world.

Toby took another flight, his laughter such a blessing.

"So what's up? Are you coming home sooner than you expected?" Leslie asked, the idea unsettling. She was enjoying her afternoons at the Dillinger's ranch more than she could have expected.

"Quite the opposite. My sister's not getting around very easily and it looks like I might need to stay longer. How are you and Seth getting along?" Claudia asked.

"Fair to middling." She'd picked up the expression somewhere along the way and it was the perfect way to describe the situation. "It was a rocky start because you forgot to call and alert Seth to the changes," Leslie said, gently admonishing the woman for the oversight. Not that it mattered now, but it had made things difficult early on.

"Oh, dear. I'm so sorry. Reckon I was beside myself with worry for my sister."

Leslie watched as Toby launched himself yet again into the air, the boy tireless in his fun. "I figured as much."

"What happened? I do know Seth's quite protective of his son."

Leslie huffed. "You can say that again. It took a little time, but Seth soon realized I was the best choice he had at his disposal."

"And now?" Claudia asked, her tone a sign she was far more interested in the answer than was called for, given Leslie was still employed as the part-time nanny.

"I think he's grateful." Especially given she'd saved Toby's birthday, but she wouldn't be sharing that information with Claudia. Information in Crossroads Creek had a way of traveling like a wildfire, and she didn't want to drop trouble at Seth's doorstep from disapproving town folk.

"*Hmmm*, perhaps more than grateful. One can hope. You know, he might make a fine husband. Easy on the eye if you know what I mean." Claudia chuckled.

Now she understood Claudia's angle. "Don't start that. You sound just like Beth." Leslie made sure Toby wasn't listening to a word she said, but also tried not to use specific words to tip the kid off and catch his interest.

"Beth's a good girl. Smart too. What's wrong with the cowboy?" Claudia asked.

Why did everyone want to connect the dots between her and Seth? "Let's just say the man wears a no trespassing sign like a second skin."

"If you say so, but people change. And I noticed you didn't say you weren't interested. Perhaps me staying in Austin longer will give the two of you time to change your minds."

A car door slammed. Leslie wasn't expecting anyone, but they did need to go see who had arrived. "Thanks for the update, Claudia, but I've got to run. We've got visitors." Leslie hung up the phone, grateful for the ability to ring off and not continue the conversation.

"Toby, we need to head for the main house. Someone's here. Might be a delivery your dad forgot to tell me about," Leslie said, tucking the phone in her pocket.

"Awww, shucks. Can't I stay and play?" he whined.

"Maybe we can come back later. But for now, you have to come with me. I'll go down first and you follow right behind me. Okay?"

"Yeah," he mumbled.

Leslie made her way down the ladder, Toby right behind her. She was relieved when they were both standing firmly on the ground. They walked quickly to the front of the house, Leslie surprised to discover a man peeking in the front windows.

"Excuse me. Can I help you?" she asked, moving in front of Toby protectively. The man looked friendly enough in his well-worn jeans and cowboy hat, but friends didn't go snooping in other people's houses.

The man grinned. "You sure can, little lady. Forgive me for peeking in the windows. I knocked, and no one answered. The front door was open, so I was trying to see if someone was inside and didn't hear me knocking."

It was a plausible excuse. "We were in the barn." The man had an easy charm, but it was his face and eyes that held her attention. He looked familiar, but she couldn't figure out why.

"Are you the lady of the house?" he asked, his gaze dropping to her left hand and then back at her.

"No. I'm Toby's teacher and I take care of him after school while Mr. Dillinger is working." She didn't owe the man any explanation but saw no harm in the truth.

The man drew back, his brow drawn tight. "Mr. Dillinger, you say? Odd to hear my son referred to as mister. That has always been my title, and my father's before me."

Son. "By son, do you mean Seth?" Leslie asked, scrunching her brow as she tried to understand the man's cryptic comment.

He nodded, his easy smile firmly back in place. "Yes. Seth Dillinger is my son and I understand he's living here now."

"Then you're his—"

"Father. Robert Dillinger. And if the young lad half tucked behind you is Seth's son, that makes him my grandson."

"He is Seth's son, yes." Leslie confirmed Toby's identity, but she wasn't ready to accept everything Robert said. That would be up to Seth to confirm.

Toby stepped forward, clearly intrigued.

Robert moved closer and kneeled down to Toby's level. "Hi there, young man. What's your name? I'm your Grandpa Dillinger."

Toby's eyes were wide as saucers. "I'm Toby and I just turned seven. I'm in first grade. Are you really my grandpa? I didn't know I had one."

"That makes us even because I didn't know about you either. You're the spitting image of your father when he was seven." The man seemed to drift down memory lane for a second, a pained expression on his face.

Leslie suddenly realized why the man looked so familiar. Seth, Toby, and Robert all had the exact same shade of chocolate eyes with gold flecks in them, brown hair, and a firm jaw. There was clearly some level of truth to what Robert claimed. "So what can we do for you, Mr. Dillinger? Seth didn't say anything about your arrival?" In fact, he'd never mentioned his father. *Ever.* And Leslie had a pretty good idea of why after talking with Claudia.

"I wanted to surprise Seth. As to the purpose of my visit...let's just say I want to reconnect with my son. Seth and I have business to discuss." There was a sudden intensity in Robert's expression that set Leslie on edge.

Once Seth got home, perhaps she would have a better understanding of the situation. "I see. Well then, won't you come in for a cup of tea, while I start to fix dinner? Seth should be home in about an hour." She'd keep a close eye on the guy for sure, but the resemblance was too strong to ignore. *Love thy neighbor*, came to mind. He wasn't a neighbor, more like family. Possibly. Almost certainly. She wouldn't turn him out until she had reason to believe he was up to no good.

"Sounds like a plan to me. You wouldn't happen to have anything stronger...like a beer?" Robert asked.

Leslie shook her head. "I don't believe so. Seth doesn't drink that I know of."

"Well then, perhaps just water. Flavored and diluted tea isn't my thing," Robert said, his easy charm coming through in heaping doses.

She gestured for him to enter the house, following him inside and keeping Toby close to her. He glanced all around the room, almost as though he were taking stock of the place. He was outgoing and friendly, unlike his son, but there was something in his attitude that seemed over the top. Almost like forced charm.

Leslie would keep her guard up until Seth arrived home, and she was able to get a read between the two men regarding the unexpected visit. She hoped this would be a happy reunion, and that she wasn't crossing any lines inviting the man inside to wait for his arrival.

The last thing she needed to do was give Seth a real reason to dislike her. Because truth be told, she rather liked the reserved man who was protective of his son, and who honestly just wanted to be a better dad.

Even if said man seemed almost clueless about how to pull it off.

Chapter Eleven

♥

Every muscle in Seth's body hurt. The hundred plus posts he drove into the ground were a true testament to the fact he wasn't in shape for this line of work. He'd worked out at the gym regularly in L.A, but this was different in that it was brutal on muscles previously unused. And he still needed to check on the horses before he could settle in for the night. It was a never-ending job, and one day, he hoped to look back and know it was all worth the effort.

The thought of a hot shower and some food kept him moving forward. That and some muscle ointment. Seth grimaced. He couldn't abide the smell of the stuff, but it was all bets off tonight. Pulling up to the house, he was more than a little surprised to see a battered old Buick parked out front with out of state plates. Colorado.

Having come from California, he couldn't imagine who would be here. It also meant the shower he desperately needed would have to wait. Seth pulled off his cowboy hat, brushed at the sweat of his brow with his shirt sleeve, and replaced his hat. He'd give whoever was here less than three minutes of his time, and that was being generous.

The screen door slammed into place behind him, announcing his presence as he stepped into the living room. Leslie jumped to her feet and moved to his side, her smile not the easy-going one he'd grown used to. His gaze dropped to Toby, who sat at the coffee table coloring a picture, his concentrated effort to stay in the lines superseding the awareness his father had arrived home.

"I'm so glad you're here," Leslie said, her voice a little strained, the tone in direct contrast to her smile.

Seth's gaze slid to the visitor at the far corner of the room. The man was sitting in the oversized recliner chair, his lounged position one of overall comfort. Clearly he had been here a while. But more than that, the man seemed vaguely familiar.

Seth frowned and took a step closer. "I'm worn out and not really in the mood for visitors," he said pointedly, hoping the man would take a hint, state his business, and leave.

The guy stood, matching Seth's height and stature.

Leslie moved closer to Seth. "But this is a very special visitor and I wouldn't let him leave until you got home and decided what to do," she said. "Don't you recognize him?" she asked, gazing back and forth between the two men.

Seth froze. Recognize him? How could he not...the brown eyes with gold in them were the same eyes he saw in the mirror every morning, and of the man in the picture Seth had kept hidden in a drawer for ten years before he had torn it up and thrown it in the trash. *His father.*

The last man he ever expected to see again. Or wanted to see again, for that matter. "What do you want?" Seth growled, skipping any form of nice formalities. His father hadn't thought twice about the wife and son he left behind when he ran off to do whatever he'd been doing all these years. He didn't deserve anything from Seth, not even kindness.

"Now is that any way to greet your old man?" Robert said, his gravelly voice and choice of words most irritating.

"Toby, can you go start your bath?" Seth asked, using a tone of voice that brooked no opposition.

"But we haven't eaten dinner." His son looked between him and his grandfather, confused by the request.

"Change of schedule for tonight," Seth said, unwilling to have Toby around for this part of the conversation.

"Yes, sir," he mumbled and walked off down the hall.

Seth turned back to his father. "If you were looking for some big fanfare greeting now that you've shown your face around these parts, you were sadly mistaken. I'm not sure why you're here, but I reckon you ought to say your peace and leave. I'm tired and four a.m. comes early."

"Seth," Leslie said, reaching out to touch his arm. "He just came to see you and talk. Maybe you should give him a chance. Toby really enjoyed having his *grandfather* around and is even working on a picture for him."

He couldn't help but notice her subtle emphasis on the word grandfather, but the man hadn't been much of a father, and certainly didn't deserve the title of grandfather. He turned back to Robert. "So talk."

"I had hoped you'd be a little more open to my being here," Robert said, without a trace of remorse in his expression. "You were too young to understand what happened, and I figure I did you a favor by leaving in the long run."

He couldn't believe that his father would have the audacity to act like everything he had done was for Seth's good. "How so?"

"Leslie was telling me you were a big city attorney...that's something you wouldn't have been able to do sticking around this backwoods town. You might have ended up just like me, changing jobs all the time and earning next to nothing. Crossroads Creek doesn't have much to offer."

Seth shot Leslie a glance and shook his head, not liking the idea she'd been telling his old man about him. Robert didn't need to know anything, just like Seth didn't want to know anything about the man standing five feet away. "And yet, here I am in this backwoods town anyway," he said, unable to keep the derision out of his voice. "You could have worked the ranch with Grandpa Dillinger."

Robert laughed. "Ah yes, my father. The man who disowned me after your mother and I split up."

Seth bristled in defense of his grandfather. He understood Lloyd Dillinger's actions more so now than ever before. "Let's cut the small talk and get to the point."

Robert cast a glance at Leslie and hesitated. "Sorry, but what I have to say is private. Do you mind giving us a minute?" he asked, his sugar sweet voice loaded with charm when addressing Leslie.

"Why, of course, Robert. I imagine the two of you have some catching up to do. You two boys play nice while I go look in on Toby and get dinner on the table." Leslie shot Seth a smile.

One he wasn't inclined to return. She was overstepping her bounds on a situation she knew nothing about. *Again.* After she disappeared, Seth turned back to his dad. "So what's the big private discussion we need to have twenty-two years after you walked out of my life, and I might add, brought you all the way from Colorado?"

Robert hesitated, his expression unreadable. Gone was the charming smile, replaced by a high level of tension and wariness in his eyes. "The ranch."

"What about the ranch?" Seth snapped, instantly on alert.

"There's no easy way to say this, so I'll come right out and get to the point. The ranch belongs to me," Robert said, pulling an envelope from his back pocket and holding it out.

Seth was reeling from the bomb his father dropped, trying to regroup. "Impossible. Grandma and Grandpa Dillinger left the place to me. They wrote you and mom out of the will not long after you left. They disowned you...their words, not mine." He still remembered how upset and hurt they had been when Robert left, his wandering eyes and lust for other women repugnant.

"Well, I have a copy of my father's will that was drafted five years ago, right before they died, which supersedes the one you would have. I reckon my father forgave me after all. Must have slipped his mind not to tell you," Robert said, smoothly trying to explain the validity of the document he still held.

Too smoothly. "Nope, not a chance. You left, and he was furious and unforgiving. He blamed you for the divorce, and for not honoring your marital commitments to remain faithful."

Robert flinched. "They seem to have told you an awful lot...you were just a boy. And clearly, didn't understand the situation."

"That's twice you've hinted about my lack of understanding, but trust me, I understood everything. Maybe not at first, but years later when I learned the truth about you and that other woman," Seth said, unwilling to give an inch to the man standing in front of him. A man he wanted gone.

"That was a long time ago, and changes nothing in the end. The ranch belongs to me. And in time, I'll leave it to you. But right now, I need a place to stay and I'm coming home. *To my home.*" Robert tossed the envelope on the coffee table.

"Except it's not your home and you're not welcome here. It's all too convenient that you show up unexpectedly five years later with an alternate version of the will. You need to hit the road back to wherever you came from and leave us alone."

"I'm not leaving. I'll take this to the local magistrate's office and we can see what he has to say about it. The place has been clearly left to ruin for a long time. Not the image of a caring landowner who believes in his ownership, if you ask me."

"No one is asking you. There is a statute of limitations that needs to be addressed with your claim as well. I only arrived a little over a month ago and it will take time and hard work to fix the place up, something you would know nothing about." What if Robert was telling the truth? Seth was reeling from the possible impact. They would have no home. No life here or anywhere. Talk about getting kicked in the teeth when he was already down. "As an attorney, you can be sure I'll look into the matter thoroughly. I won't just walk away on your say so...that's your specialty."

Robert flinched. "Suit yourself. That's your copy," he said, pointing to the envelope on the table. "Seth...I can't undo the past, and I'm sorry about all this. But this is my home where I grew up, and right now, this is what I want and need. And I have every right to it," he said, delivering the final comment with a steadfast assurance that surprised him.

Seth, on the other hand, figured this is what his father needed until the next fancy skirt claimed his attention and he walked away once again. And then what happened to the ranch? His old man couldn't keep up with the place and judging by the battered car with its faded and peeling paint, Robert didn't have a penny to his name or the means to fix it up.

And there was no way Seth and Toby would be sticking around if his father took control. But for now, it would seem he didn't have much choice in the matter. "Do what you got to do, and I'll do what I have to do. I imagine we can figure out how best to avoid each other. I don't want you filling Toby's head with any "grandparent" ideas or grand schemes to disillusion him when you leave again." It also left in question what would happen to the loan on the property if the collateral never turned out to be Seth's. As an attorney, he knew there were all sorts of issues that would arise as to the legalities. Worst case scenario, Seth was left holding the bag on a large debt.

Robert nodded. "He's a fine-looking young man. You've got to know I wouldn't hurt him."

"I know nothing of the sort. Now that we've set up some ground rules, I need to shower, eat, and hit the sack. So it's time you left." It was the nicest way he could find to tell his father to get out.

"About that..." Robert paused. Shifting his weight to the opposite side, while glancing at the wall to Seth's right, as though interested in the black stallion painting that hung there. Octavius had been a legend in his time, the star of the Dillinger Equine Center. The horse had a pedigree beyond compare and numerous foals who went on to become famous show jumpers. "Any chance you'll let me sleep in the bunkhouse? I need a place to stay."

Leslie walked back into the room. "Sleep in the bunkhouse? Surely not, Seth. He's your father. And there's plenty of food for dinner for everyone."

Seth shook his head. "Stay out of what doesn't concern you, Leslie." He rubbed his head, trying to decide. He was tired of fighting this battle and nothing would be solved tonight. "Fine. But just a couple of nights till you find a place in town and figure things out."

Robert smiled, the look of relief on his face clear. "Leslie, don't worry about dinner for me. I heard the community center in town has free meals for everyone and I thought I'd check it out. And thanks for letting me stay, son."

"Don't go there," Seth warned. He couldn't believe he'd agreed to let Robert stay. The only plausible explanation was his exhaustion. That and Leslie's frown of disapproval when she realized he was about to kick his father to the curb.

"There's blankets and sheets out in the bunkhouse. Now, if you don't mind..." he added, hoping his father would take the hint and leave so that he could eat, shower, and sleep.

"Say no more," Robert said, suddenly showing signs of fatigue as though emotionally drained.

The door closed behind his father, leaving Leslie and Seth alone.

"That was the right choice," Leslie said, breaking the silence.

Seth shook his head, trying not to blame her for this next upheaval in his life. "Probably not, but what's done is done."

"He's your father," she said softly.

Busybody in action. "He's also the man trying to take the ranch from me."

Leslie sucked in a deep breath. "I'm so sorry. I had no idea. In hindsight, I should have never let him in, but I kept thinking maybe whatever happened between you two might get resolved.

You know, closure on a past that has the power to hurt you."

Seth pinned her with a gaze before forcing a slight smile to his lips. "Exactly why you should let me handle my own business." It was the truth, but he wouldn't be a bear about pointing out the obvious. Not with Leslie, who had done nothing but shower him with kindness every step of the way...whether he wanted her help or not.

"Point taken. But consider this...Toby really likes his grandfather. It could be the very thing your son needs as a positive focus in his life. New family to replace what he lost when his parents divorced," she said, jumping right back in to the thick of things.

Seth should have known she wouldn't back down. "I'm the family Toby needs and the two of us are going to be just fine, no matter where we end up living when all this is over. That is, if you stop inviting strangers into the house and trying to make everyone play nice when the playground is closed."

"There's nothing wrong with playing nice. And if you keep a positive attitude and pray about all this, perhaps you might even make peace with the past. Something both you and Toby need desperately."

Seth knew Leslie was right but admitting it to her was out of the question. He would never get rid of the meddling teacher.

Chapter Twelve

♥

OVER THE PAST COUPLE of days, Leslie had done her best to not only keep a protective eye on Toby, but both of the Dillinger men as well. Robert's charm seemed somewhat artificial. But then, what did she expect from the man trying to take his son's ranch? And therein lay the problem...was he a good guy or a bad guy? If he legitimately owned the ranch, she could understand his point of view. And so far, she had heard nothing more on the subject. The men were private about the whole affair, the tension thick and stifling when they were in the same room.

Something Toby had noticed and questioned her about this morning at school. Whatever the results between the two men, Toby was caught in the middle. *Again.*

It wasn't fair to the kid, and like it or not, she intended to fix the problem. Or *try* to fix it. With careful planning, she made dinner, sending invitations to both men, and hoping neither would cry off when they realized what she had done. Based on her text, they would both assume the invitation included Toby and herself, but Leslie had no intention of sticking around. The robust spaghetti and garlic bread for three remarks had been intentional, designed to throw them off, and it had worked.

Robert normally took off to eat somewhere else, returning late and always after she was gone. What happened after that was anyone's guess. Seth and Toby ate right when he got home, the man hungry as a bottomless pit, or so it would seem. There were never any leftovers. So either he was famished or he liked her cooking—or a bit of both.

"I'm glad you're staying for supper, Robert," Leslie said when he walked into the kitchen.

Robert smiled and lifted the cover off the sauce pot on the stove, inhaling the garlic and tomato aroma. "Couldn't turn down the chance for a home-cooked meal with you and my grandson. Where's Seth anyway? On another horse buying expedition?" The man was trying to be nonchalant but missed the mark.

Leslie shrugged. "I'm not sure where he is," she hedged, not bothering to correct the older man. "Are you feeling okay? Your face is quite pale." It wasn't the first time she noticed he looked worn out.

"I'm fine," Robert huffed. "Just all this ranch business is wearing me out."

She didn't want the man fired up before her grand plan for the evening was revealed or Robert would be out the door lickety-split. "I'm sure you understand this is Seth and Toby's home currently. You can't expect them to just pack up and leave when you show up. Give this time to get settled."

"No, but I'm tired of being on the road and without my own place. The ranch is a safe haven for me, and I need it more than Seth. Besides, there is no reason they can't stay here with me. They are my family. My *only* family."

"Have you said as much to him yet?" she asked, fairly certain Robert hadn't breathed a word of it to Seth. Otherwise, Seth would have probably mentioned it by now.

"No. My son hates me and the last thing he'll want to do is stick around if I'm in residence. But it will be his choice to leave this time. Not mine." Robert let out a deep sigh, as though it was all too much.

"You should talk to him," Leslie said softly. The men clearly needed someone to push them in the right direction if they ever planned to have an open discussion about the past. Anything would be better than the complete discord and avoidance presented to each other currently.

Robert leaned back against the counter, a thoughtful expression on his face as he watched her stir the sauce. "Wouldn't do any good if Seth's not listening. Trust me, I know my son all too well. He's a younger version of me. And no one could tell me a thing when I was his age. Or even when I got older. Thought I knew it all and didn't need anyone."

The regret was clear, but it was more than that. Guilt, perhaps? "I'm guessing it hasn't been all sunshine and roses for you."

"More like weeds and thorns. But a man has his pride, at least he does, until life forces him to see things differently."

Now they were getting somewhere. "What has forced—"

"Want to play chess, Grandpa?" Toby asked, joining them in the kitchen.

"Sure thing," Robert answered quickly, suddenly all smiles for his grandson. The man enjoyed spending time with Toby and teaching him the game, even if Toby was a bit young. Occasionally, Robert even let his grandson win.

It was the mark of a good man. Maybe one who took some wrong turns in life, but is still a good person deep down. Perhaps forgiveness was in order all the way around to help the

Dillinger's find peace with the past. For now, any answers she was about to get were forgotten.

The back door opened and Seth walked in. "*Mmmm*. Smells good in here."

"Thanks. Lots of fresh garlic and tomatoes has a way of doing that," she teased.

"Dinner almost ready? You said five o'clock sharp and I didn't want to be late." He glanced at his watch as though to confirm he was on time.

"I'm about to serve. Go wash up, and yes, your timing is perfect."

Seth rinsed his hands in the kitchen sink. "I was surprised you were staying for dinner, but I know how happy it will make Toby. Seems odd for you to fix dinner for us and then have to go home and fix dinner for yourself. This makes way more sense."

Leslie flushed with pleasure at the comment. If she didn't misunderstand him, he actually wanted her to join them for dinner on a regular basis. Something to think about later, but not now. Not tonight. "Oh, but I'm not staying."

"But you said three," Seth said, his brow tightly drawn.

Time to test the waters. "Yes. You, Toby, and your father."

Seth shook his head. "No way. It's out of the question. I'm not breaking bread with the man who broke my mother's heart. Not to mention my grandparent's hearts." His easy-going attitude vanished in the space of a second.

"Listen to me for a minute. While your father's here, you need to try to let the past...well, stay in the past. People change. Give him a chance. If not for your sake, do it for Toby. Please," she added, reaching out to touch his arm, urging him to understand.

He glanced down at her hand and stepped away. "He's trying to take the ranch from me and you're still insisting I play nice. What gives?"

It was time for Seth to face the facts. "Yes, I do. If the ranch is truly his, then he deserves it.

And vice versa. But Toby also deserves his family...and that includes his grandfather. The two get along quite well when you're not around."

"Which is exactly why I didn't want him staying here in the first place." He let out a deep sigh. "So my father is here now? Is that what you're telling me? I've got too much on my plate to deal with him."

Leslie nodded. "Yes. He's in the front room playing chess with Toby."

"The kid is too young to understand the game."

"Maybe, maybe not. Depends on the child. But Toby craves the attention he's getting, so I can tell he's trying really hard. Your dad makes him feel special and wanted simply by spending time with him...and having fun."

Seth quirked up one eyebrow. "Another shot at my inability to do the same?"

Leslie shrugged. She was poking the bear...but this Papa bear needed a shove in the right direction. "Not a shot. Simple truth."

"Fine. I'll do the whole dinner thing on one condition."

His smirk made her wary, but she had to ask. "What's that?"

"You stay. I'm sure we'll need a referee and I have it on good authority you can handle the job."

"But I—"

"No buts. You stay or I go...take your pick."

Seth had her cornered on this request and he knew it. "Fine, I'll stay. Like you said, it will save me from having to cook dinner a second time later tonight." What he didn't know was that she fully intended to put the time to good use and move them toward some sort of reconciliation laced with forgiveness.

It would be a powerful lesson for Toby, but more importantly, a powerful impact on the kid's sense of family and belonging, something he desperately needed.

Seth headed down the hall to finish getting cleaned up for supper. Much to his dismay, he had been looking forward to dinner with the pretty teacher and his son. There was never a dull moment when she was around, even if he disagreed with her interference. It certainly kept him on his toes and thinking of new ways to make Toby happy.

Which is exactly why he had enrolled his son at the Devoe Ranch for riding lessons. Rusty Devoe was highly recommended as a retired bull rider and Seth felt his son would be in excellent hands. To top off what he assumed would be a well-received gift, Seth had also bought Toby a saddle, boots, cowboy hat, a helmet and all the clothes he might need to help him fit right in with the image. His son would be over the moon, and not even Robert's presence would ruin this moment for Seth.

After a quick shave and washing his face, he stopped at the dresser. With only the slightest hesitation, he splashed on some cologne. Not to impress his female guest, but as a courtesy in case there were any lingering odors from a day on the ranch. Contrary to what she thought, he wasn't a total barbarian.

Arriving at the dining room, his gaze landed on his father. The man had the audacity to sit at the head of the table...in Seth's normal spot. Seth clenched his jaw, trying to decide what to do. "You know, you're sitting—"

"At the head of the table where he belongs. There are two heads at a table and only two of you. I guess that makes it easy to figure out the seating arrangements," Leslie said, shooting Seth a wink to take the edge out of her comment. *And to change the outcome.*

"Yes, it would seem so," he agreed. Seth held out a chair for Leslie before taking his own seat.

Robert started to rise. "I didn't know you were joining us," he said, a frown marring his face.

"Sit down, Robert," Leslie ordered, brooking no opposition.

When his father sat back down, it surprised Seth. "That makes two of us not in the loop. It would seem Leslie managed to set this up all on her own. Good thing I made her stay for dinner."

"I agree," Robert said with a shake of his head.

"It's the first and last thing we'll probably agree on, but it's a start," Seth taunted, knowing his chat with an attorney from Dallas today brought some good insights as to state law and estates. Not that he would be giving away any information to his father. Not yet anyway.

"This will be the best dinner ever. My dad, my grandpa, and my teacher are all here. My three favorite people. And after dinner, we can all watch a movie or play games," Toby beamed, looking around the table for confirmation.

"Let's just get through dinner," Seth said, dishing out a kid-size portion on his son's plate before adding a heaping pile to his own. He passed the bowl to Leslie, and soon, everyone's plate was loaded with pasta and the fresh spaghetti sauce he couldn't wait to taste. It had been a childhood favorite of his when he visited the ranch. His grandmother's garden was always brimming over with fresh vegetables, and the woman was a master in the kitchen. It was a shame he hadn't learned anything from her, as it would have come in handy cooking meals for Toby. Instead, processed dinners and canned goods had been at the top of his list, at least until Leslie started cooking for them. He shook the parmesan cheese generously on top of his spaghetti before passing it to Leslie.

"Let's say grace before we eat," Leslie said, stopping the men with their forks mid-air.

Something Seth hadn't done at mealtimes since he left home, but he remembered all too well from his past. His grandparents always said grace before the meal.

"There comes a time in a man's life when he doesn't necessarily find that sort of thing means anything, but knock yourself out," Robert said, shaking his head, his face void of emotion.

"I like talking to God because he makes me smile," Toby said, his expression far too serious as he gazed at his grandfather.

"When I was your age, it made me smile. People grow up and change," Robert said.

It was a hint of the past, but his father had been in control of his own destiny. The same way Seth was now. Only his choice hadn't been to walk away from Toby, but to embrace his son and do right by him. A character quality his father had been sadly lacking. "And some don't," he offered.

"And some people grow up and still love talking to God. I'm one of them," Leslie said, joining into the controversial subject.

"What about you, Dad? Do you like talking to God?" Toby asked.

Seth sat back in his chair, not at all prepared for the question. "The jury is still out." Actually, the jury had decided, but he wasn't willing to douse his son's faith as a result. If there was a God, why then was Toby left motherless when Alicia walked out of his life? Why had Seth's law firm closed its doors before he ever made partner? And even now, if his own father had a choice, he would take the very home and ranch where Seth lived right out from under them. It was one thing after another and there was no relief in sight.

In the meantime, his food was growing cold. "Go ahead, Leslie."

"Thank you. Father God, I ask that you bless the time Seth and Robert have together and with Toby, and that you show them a way to make things right and add peace into their lives and hearts. And I ask that you bless this food for the nourishment of our bodies and souls. Amen."

"Amen," Seth uttered. Blessing the food was one thing, but as to her first request...Leslie didn't understand and would be less than happy with the outcome if he had his way and his father was sent packing.

All four of them started eating, conversation limited to a few *please pass* and *thank you* tidbits.

"So what did you do today, Robert?" Leslie asked, breaking the strained silence.

"Not much. Ran into Austin this morning and then hung out around here. Not much else I can do, I reckon. Not till things are settled," he added, sending Seth a pointed look.

Seth hadn't planned on bringing up the subject, but Robert had stepped right into the cow patty on this one. "Well, it might not be much longer. I talked to the district attorney, and he seems to think the odds of the will you have being legitimate are slim to none. The estate was properly advertised and settled by a trustee and executor, and based on the information at the time, I own the place."

Robert frowned. "But my copy of the will is dated after yours."

"True, but it doesn't automatically make it legal," Seth said, not bothering to hide behind any innuendo of dirty dealings.

"Are you insinuating I'd try to do something illegal and steal the place from my one and only son?"

It was a good act, but Seth wasn't buying into it. "Not insinuating anything. Just saying I have to look at all possibilities, that being one of them. There's a lot at stake. Texas law allows for a review of the will, but how and when you came into possession of it will be thoroughly reviewed." Not to mention the loan aspect, but he wouldn't be saying a word about it to Robert. It was none of his business. Yet.

"I don't have to put up with this," Robert said, tossing his napkin on the table and rising.

"Robert, please don't go," Leslie said, looking back and forth between the men.

"I don't see as I have much of a choice. I'll be in the bunkhouse if you need me. Thanks for a lovely meal." Robert turned and walked out, without so much as a backward glance at Seth. Or Toby.

So much for Leslie running interference.

"Well, that didn't go as planned. You could have kept quiet about your findings until a more private moment to discuss them," Leslie said, her voice clipped as though she'd run out of patience.

That made two of them. "Or I could have not been forced to eat a meal with my father and then none of this would have happened."

"*Arghhh.* You're both so stubborn, and far more alike than either of you will ever admit."

"I'm nothing like him." Except the problem was...in a way...she was right. No he hadn't walked out on his son, or anything like that...but he was part in parcel a reason for the failed marriage. He and Alicia had never even considered the negative impact of providing the perfect family unit for the job. The only thing they saw was a partnership, power, money...and prestige.

"Why do you two have to argue all the time? Grandpa was supposed to stay and play games with us tonight." Toby scowled, looking far more like Seth and his father than he cared to admit. "You're not going to leave too, are you Miss Sullivan?" Toby added.

Leslie hesitated, then shook her head. "No way. And miss all the fun? Not to mention, dessert."

"Yay. I didn't know we had dessert. What is it?" he asked, his bright smile firmly back in place.

"Peach Melba. It's peaches and a special syrup drizzled over French vanilla ice cream," Leslie explained, rising to pick up the plates from the table.

"That sounds delish. And then we can watch a movie, right?" Toby asked.

Leslie shrugged. "It depends on what you and your father want."

"Can we, dad? Can we?" Toby asked, hope dripping from each plea.

There was no way Seth would ruin the evening. His father had taken those honors, storming out the way he did. He hadn't accused his dad of anything, only clued him in with a dose of reality. Besides, he rather enjoyed Leslie's company.

At least some of the time, he corrected. "Sure thing. And I've got a couple of surprises for you too, Toby," he added, remembering the gifts he picked up in town today when he ran a couple of errands.

Toby's face lit up, and the kid was suddenly at full attention, eager to find out what he meant. "For me? Why? It's not my birthday. I just had one."

Seth grinned. "No, but any day is a good day for a dad to give his son a gift." *Or gifts, he corrected.* Money was tight when it came to the expenses for the horses, but a few gifts here and there could hardly compare or make a difference to the success or failure of the ranch.

"All right. I can't wait to see what you bought." Toby beamed.

The sound of a car accelerating away from the house caught his attention. So his dad wasn't retiring to the bunkhouse. Just like all the other nights and most days, he spent his time away from the ranch. Seth didn't have a clue where he went or what he did, but doubted the old man was up to any good.

It might prove beneficial to keep a closer eye on his dad, just in case.

Chapter Thirteen

♥

LESLIE HEARD THE SAME sound Seth had and wondered at his father's hasty departure. Her plan to help the two of them move past some of their differences had backfired. But at least Seth hadn't sent her packing. Instead, they were going to have movie night.

The dishes were all done, and she re-entered the living room, setting the dessert tray on the coffee table. Her gaze shifted to Toby, the kid over-the-top excited with a mass of new gifts all around him. Seth had mentioned a few—but this was significantly more than that.

"Look, Miss Sullivan," Toby said, holding up each gift for her inspection. "Aren't these cool? And wait until you hear the best part. I'm going to learn to ride. Starting when Miss Claudia gets back from her sisters so she can take me. My dad's the best dad ever."

It was like Christmas in September. "Wow. What a surprise. That sounds like super-duper fun. And I love your new cowboy hat and boots," Leslie said, infusing enthusiasm into her voice. There was also a belt, jeans, a vest, a belt buckle, riding gloves, a bandana, and what looked to be two or three new shirts. Seth had gone over the top with his gifts, but judging from his self-satisfied expression, the man was pleased with the result.

The problem was that Toby's super-high would only last as long as the gifts were new and a novelty. Riding lessons were a great idea, but Leslie couldn't help but wonder why Seth wouldn't teach his own son, considering the man rode like he had been born in the saddle even after a lengthy time away from the ranch. Seth was a natural. Teaching his son would have been a better way to connect and forge a more lasting bond between them.

Toby ran around the room, pretending to ride, his laughter music to Leslie's ears. Temporary, yes, but still good.

"I figured any kid that lived on a ranch should know how to ride," Seth said by way of explanation.

"True," Leslie said, shooting him a soft smile. "So, what's on tap for the movie?"

"Can we watch Hotel Transylvania?" Toby asked, coming to stand next to her as he eyeballed the desserts.

"Your choice is fine by me," Leslie said, setting his Peach Melba in front of him on the coffee table. "Be careful and lean over," she cautioned.

"*Hmmm*, this is sooo good," Toby exclaimed, taking another bite.

"And here's yours, Seth." Leslie handed him one of the desserts and then proceeded to dig into her own. She loved the rich, fresh peach flavor laced with a raspberry sauce. It had always been one of her favorites, but then, ice cream made just about anything a favorite.

"This is really good," Seth said, echoing his son's opinion.

Leslie flushed with pleasure, happy to have come up with a winning dessert. "Thank you. I'm glad you like it."

Seth stood and moved to the TV, firing up the DVD as they all settled in to watch. The movie turned out to be one more geared for Toby with the monsters in action, not something Leslie could find a way to get into.

Instead, she spent more time thinking about and observing Seth and his son, worrying over how to fix the damage she'd done tonight between Seth and Robert.

Something would have to give soon. The problem was, no matter the outcome of the legalities of the will Robert had, someone would be left out in the cold. And she couldn't bring herself to believe it should be Seth and Toby.

If only she could understand either one of the men more, then perhaps she could figure a way to help them work through the past. But they were both a closed book to the outside world. Like father, like son in so many ways. Not that she'd point that out to Seth because he certainly wouldn't consider it a good thing.

By the time the movie was finished, Leslie was no closer to figuring anything out than when she started.

Toby yawned.

"Time for bed, young man," Seth said.

"Do I have to?" Toby whined, sounding more like a six-year-old than seven. Which was exactly what happened when a kid got overtired.

Seth nodded, giving his son a gentle push in the right direction. "Absolutely. Brush your teeth and get your pajamas on. I'll be in shortly to tuck you in."

"Okay," Toby mumbled. "Bye, Miss Sullivan. I loved your dessert and I hope you make it again for me soon."

"Goodnight, Toby," Leslie said, giving the boy a hug.

"I can't wait until after school Monday so I can play with Jelly again."

The mention of her dog served as a reminder Leslie needed to get a move on herself and let the dog out. "I'm sure Jelly is looking forward to playing with you, too."

Toby walked down the hall and disappeared from view.

"I think my son's going to be very upset to not have you all to himself after school when Claudia gets back. He's quite attached, you know."

"I think he's pretty special. But on the subject of Claudia, I forgot to tell you she called the other day. In all the excitement of your father's arrival, I failed to tell you that she thinks it might be another week or so. Which is fine by me, but probably not so fine by Toby if it means he doesn't get to start his lessons anytime soon. I don't mind taking him, you know."

"I just didn't want to ask you to do more than you already have."

"I'll let you know when you're crossing the line, mister," she said, laughing up at him.

Seth grinned and nodded. "In that case...I guess it will be okay. I'll try to set it up with

Rusty tomorrow and let you know what he says."

"Out of curiosity, why aren't you teaching Toby? It would mean more and give you a chance to spend time with him. Time he needs and seems to enjoy so much, I might add."

"Unfortunately, time is something I don't have. Besides, that would require more money to buy a pleasure horse, a luxury I can't afford right now. Horses are expensive and I've put everything I have into getting the ranch back in business."

"I understand. It just seems such a shame." She shrugged. "Let me run the dessert dishes to the sink and I'll see my way out."

"I'll take care of it." Seth walked her to the front door.

"Okay, then. Thanks. I'll see you tomorrow." She reached for her sweater and started to pull it on. The collar twisted under the neckline and Seth moved closer, trying to fix it.

"It's chilly out there tonight," he said, trying unsuccessfully to cover the move, his face flushing a couple of shades of pink.

Interesting. "Yes, it's supposed to get down in the sixties."

They stepped out onto the porch. Leslie turned back to say goodnight, instead running smack dab into the man's rock-solid chest.

"Sorry," Leslie mumbled. This time she was the one trying to cover an awkward move, but at least he couldn't see the warm flush she felt covering her own face, not with the moonlight at her back.

Seth leaned forward slightly, time stopping as he closed the distance between them.

It suddenly dawned on Leslie that he was about to kiss her...something she shouldn't let happen. Her mind raced as though time had stopped. Student-Parent. Handsome cowboy. Who was he to her, and what should she do about it?

Seth touched her face, his mouth inches from hers, the same indecision etched across his features.

"Dad, are you coming?" Toby hollered.

Student-Parent. That was the final answer for them both.

Seth dropped his hand and moved away. "I'm sorry." He turned and headed inside, leaving her with a heaping dose of regret for one.

The almost kiss was telling. Luckily, Seth had his priorities straight, because Leslie was pretty sure she would have let him kiss her. Something that would have caused far more problems than she was prepared to handle. Yes, the rules. But also the man.

Emotionally unavailable. Tonight was probably nothing more than moonlight magic.

It would be all too easy to fall for the handsome cowboy and for all the wrong reasons. Her desire for a family. She couldn't have kids and Toby was so darn cute and loveable. But it wasn't enough to base a marriage. Mutual goals that had nothing to do with love. Not to mention the man himself on more than one occasion had made his feelings about her quite clear.

NI. *Kid talk for not interested.*

Chapter Fourteen

♥

TOBY WAS READY FOR school Monday morning...a welcome change. As he devoured his breakfast with a healthy appetite, Seth didn't bother to tell him to slow down. His son's changed attitude was proof they were moving in the right direction.

Seth took a sip of coffee and glanced at his watch. They had ten minutes before it was time to leave, but all he could think about was the horses waiting to be brushed down, fed, and watered, the work on the house, the pastures that needed checking, the barn that needed painting, and quite a few other repairs before winter arrived. Every day it seemed like his to-do list grew instead of shrinking.

"Oh, I almost forgot. Miss Coble gave us this form last week, but I keep forgetting to give it to you. She told me if I don't have you sign this, I can't go on today's field trip." Toby reached into his backpack and handed Seth a yellow paper.

"Good thing you remembered then." He glanced down at the note and started to read. It would seem they were bound for the science center today...at a cost of ten dollars per kid. And a suggested amount for lunch money and a souvenir. It all added up to twenty-five dollars, which was quite a bit of money for a first-grade school trip.

What happened to two and three dollar admissions like when he was a boy?

"Can I go?" Toby asked.

"Of course." He would never keep his son from learning opportunities, but more importantly, bonding opportunities outside of the classroom. He picked up the pen and signed the paper, folding it and handing it back to Toby. Seth reached for his wallet, only to discover he didn't have enough to cover the expense. Charge cards and debit cards had taken the place of cash, and in the city, it had never been wise to walk around with large sums of money.

He stood and made his way to the cupboard, reaching up on the top shelf to retrieve the tin coffee can where he kept extra cash. This was definitely one of those just-in-case moments. Seth pulled out the wad of cash, surprised at how little there seemed to be. Enough to give Toby, but it left to question where the rest of the money had gone.

And his thoughts landed on the most likely person—his dad. The man had nothing to his name except his car and a few boxes of clothes, judging from what Seth had seen thus far. Leslie and Toby weren't even on his radar. There had to have been well over a hundred dollars in the can. With a shake of his head, he pushed the thought away, not wanting to burden Toby with his discovery. Seth pasted on a smile and handed his son the money. "Put this in your front zipper pouch and be sure to give it to Miss Coble as soon as you get to school. If you lose it, you won't be able to go on the trip."

"Yes, sir," Toby said, tucking the money away as he was instructed.

It was a lot of cash for a seven-year-old, but then they had to start learning responsibility sometime and it was only between the truck and his classroom.

After Toby was in school, Seth planned to have a conversation with his dad. If he could find him. His father rarely hung around the ranch, or to Seth's knowledge anyway, since he was out working all day.

The man didn't mind a roof over his head, but there hadn't been a single offer to help out with the ranch chores. His focus seemed to be on Toby, which wasn't a bad thing considering he was the grandfather. It's just what would happen when the legality of the will was settled? Seth was almost positive it was a fake copy and Robert would be out of the house soon. The fact he would try to cheat Seth out of his inheritance didn't sit well either. And a man who would go to the extremes his father had gone to was certainly capable of stealing money from a tin can. Except Seth had no proof. *Not yet anyway.*

"Time to go, kiddo," Seth said, taking his bowl and rinsing it in the sink.

"Yay, I can't wait to see Ava and Lindsey. We are all gonna ride the bus together to the science center. And Miss Sullivan is going with us. She's super cool and makes everything fun."

They arrived at the school and Seth parked in the drop-off line. "Have a good day. And don't forget to give Miss Coble your money," Seth reminded him.

"Okay. Bye, Dad."

Toby was in better spirits these days, and it made things easier on Seth. The gifts he'd given his son had been a big hit, proving that they had been a good choice. And come Monday, Leslie would take him to the equestrian center for lessons.

Seth arrived back at the ranch, noting his father still wasn't around. Which was probably a good thing. He'd keep his thoughts to himself, but he'd also start paying closer attention to the unwelcome guest in his home.

The sun was setting on the horizon, a sure sign it was quitting time. A dirty mess of sweat and grime, Seth urged his horse back to the barn. The hard work wasn't as taxing on his body anymore, and it was a great source of relief for the troubles he'd gone over and over in his mind. Right now, the only thing he wanted was a shower and a full belly and some downtime.

The house was quiet when he walked in. "Anyone here?" he called out.

"In here," Leslie called out from Toby's room.

Seth made his way down the hall. "What are you—" he stopped short, seeing his dad with them.

"Look at what Grandpa bought me. Isn't it totally cool?" Toby said, pointing at the train and tracks set up. *All around the room.*

The train rode on a shelf attached to the wall halfway up around most of the room perimeter, with a steep hill to go up and over the doorway. The train moved slowly as it went through mountain passes and over bridges, stopping and starting at various points. People. A village. Everything.

A gift from his father. Seth scowled, knowing this was the proof he needed of the stolen money. The man had nothing and suddenly he's got plenty to buy Toby a gift. *An unreasonable and expensive gift.* "That's great," he lied.

"It's my birthday present since Grandpa just missed it," Toby beamed.

"That's not all that's missing around here," Seth ground out. "I'm sure you'll enjoy it" Without so much as a glance at his father for fear his anger would topple over and let loose in front of his son, he turned to leave. "I've got to get something to eat."

Footsteps on the hardwood floors alerted Seth someone had followed.

"What's wrong? You don't seem overly happy about this?" Leslie asked, catching up with him.

He huffed. "Why would I be happy about it? He's trying to buy Toby's affections." *With Seth's money at that.*

"Isn't that what you just did? You both need to grow up and figure out what Toby really needs is more time with you. You can't buy love." Leslie wasn't pulling any punches as she delivered the set down.

It irritated him more because her words were a little too close to the truth. Except that being grouped in the same category as his father didn't sit well. "Well, in my father's case, he can't even buy a gift," Seth retorted, unable to hold back the ugly truth.

Leslie grabbed his arm. "What's that supposed to mean?"

"I'm reasonably certain he stole the money from a can where I keep cash here at the ranch."

"Do you have proof? Reasonably certain isn't enough. This is your father we're talking about.

And what if it's not true? You can't go around accusing him because he bought Toby a gift. You don't know his situation. The mans a drifter, not necessarily a liar and a thief."

Leslie always tried to see the good in everyone, but this time, she was going too far. The timing was more than a little coincidental for Seth's liking. "But he could be. I, for one, will be keeping a closer eye on him, and I suggest you do the same. I don't trust the guy, whether he's my father or not. Mark my words, if anything else happens around here, I'll send him packing no matter what document he has saying the ranch is his."

Chapter Fifteen

♥

"You're a little quiet this morning, Toby. What's going on?" Seth asked. Monday the kid had been in high spirits and talking about the field trip all evening, making sure Seth learned everything Toby discovered that day. And now, only two days later...it was as though the light had gone out in his son's eyes.

Toby shrugged. "It's nothing." His son's focus was glued to his bowl of cereal, but he was picking at it, swirling the spoon in the milk, but not eating.

A definite clue something was wrong. "I know you better than that. Something's bothering you, but I can't help if you don't talk to me."

Warm brown eyes shaded with sadness landed on Seth, his son's expression more than a little troubling.

"It's about mom," Toby mumbled.

This wasn't what Seth expected at all, but perhaps he should have seen it coming. "What about her?"

"Why doesn't she ever call me? Or come to see me?" he asked, his voice dropping a notch or two.

He grasped for the right words. "People get busy. And she knows you're safe with me and that I'll take excellent care of you."

"But everyone else has a mom and dad. It's not fair."

"You're wrong. Not everyone has both, sometimes by choice, other times not. Unfortunately, divorce is a reality in our world. But when a couple splits up, they generally try to do what's best for the children. That's what I'm doing with you, and why we're in Crossroads Creek. Don't you like it here? I mean, I thought you were finally starting to fit in and making friends." Seth was counting on the question being somewhat rhetorical based on his son's new positive attitude at school this past week. Otherwise, he might have just stepped into a pile of manure.

Toby shrugged. "I guess it's good. I am making friends. And then there's Miss Sullivan. I love my teacher."

Seth let out a small sigh of relief. He understood his son's adoration of the teacher. The woman had a heart of gold and would be every child's favorite. Recalling the cake incident, he knew she truly cared about every child and went beyond the call of duty to make them feel special. "That's great. Try not to focus on what you don't have, instead counting the blessings for what you do have. I'm sure your mom will call soon."

"You think so?" Toby asked, his eyes lighting up.

"Sure. Who can resist talking to you for very long?" Seth teased. Even if the phone call required a subtle behind-the-scenes push. "Finish your breakfast and get dressed for school."

Toby drank the rest of the milk from the bowl. It wasn't exactly high society, but then they were on a ranch in the country and he was just a kid. His son always claimed the sweet milk was the best part, and who was he to stop the pleasure? Kids grew out of it, the not so perfect etiquette...eventually.

The front door opened and Robert walked in. "Hope you don't mind, but I need to shower. The hot water heater doesn't seem to be working in the bunkhouse."

No good morning. No lead in conversation. Nothing. Which was okay by Seth. "Fine. I'll see what I can do to fix it today." It was one more thing to add to his never-ending to-do list.

Seth headed for his bedroom, pulled out his phone and dialed Alicia.

"Seth? Is everything okay? It's really early and I'm not even out of bed," Alicia said, her voice groggy from sleep.

"No, everything is not okay," he said, skipping any formalities and wanting to get this conversation over with. "Toby is upset because you haven't called or come to see him. You even missed his birthday. I know you're in your own little world, but there's your son to consider, whether you like it or not." A twinge of guilt ripped through Seth, knowing he had also forgotten Toby's birthday and might be coming on a little strong. Luckily, Leslie had saved the day.

Alicia yawned. "Things are busy here. Surely you can explain it to him. I miss Toby, but I can't go backward. He has you. I've got Teddy. We got married, you know. And I'm pregnant. I'm in the first trimester and having a rough go of it. Honestly, it's about all I can handle right now."

His ex-wife had been dating Teddy Bennington III, a partner in his father's law firm. Seth wondered if the pregnancy was all part of the plan to make sure this time around that Alicia got the social status she wanted. "I won't congratulate you on getting married or getting pregnant. Not if it's at Toby's expense. I never realized how self-centered you could be."

"You always were such a bore. Just make up some excuse. It's not wrong to want nice things in life. It's who I am. Who you used to be, so don't forget that."

Seth let out a deep breath. "*Used to be* is the operative phrase. Ranching is hard work, but it could be the best thing that's ever happened to me." *That is, if his father didn't take it all away.* This place gave Seth a new lease on life, and a second chance with Toby.

"That's exactly what I'm talking about. We are two different people, so don't fault me for following my dreams. I could never take up residence on a ranch or live that kind of...*ummm*...life," Alicia said, her voice dripping with disdain.

"None of this changes the fact that you already have a son and should consider his needs."

"I have a baby on the way and my focus is on the future with my new family. Toby will be just fine with you. It would only confuse him more if I was in the picture."

Seth was growing more frustrated with each passing second. "Shallow never used to be your middle name."

"And it's not now, not the way I see it. I took care of Toby almost exclusively for the first six years, something you seem to forget. And all I got for the time and effort I put into making the right appearances and hosting parties for you, was to end up the wife of an unemployed attorney. Pardon me if I don't want to dwell on the past. I'm sure you can think of some plausible excuse. You're good at that," Alicia added, taking the shot without so much as a hint of remorse.

The problem was, she was right. His entire focus had been on making partner, sacrificing family time to get ahead. "Fine, I'll figure something out to tell him." Or perhaps he should buy something for Toby when he broke the news. The kid liked gifts, and it worked well last time. Including his grandfather's somewhat dubious origins gift. Seth disconnected the phone, hurrying out of the bedroom to find Toby and take him to school. He practically crashed into his father in front of the bathroom.

Robert drew up a short, painful expression on his face. "I'm done. Thanks." He wrapped the towel around his shoulders.

Seth's gaze landed on his father's arms, the T-shirt he wore exposing the flesh normally covered by a long-sleeve shirt. The marks on his arms weren't hard to figure out, but of all the things he could have imagined, his father as a drug addict wasn't one of them. He grabbed his father's arm. "What are these?" he asked.

Robert pulled away. "None of your business," he snapped.

"It's my business when you're around Toby every day. I don't want a drug user in my house, so I think you should start talking or get out." He was done trying to do the right thing because, clearly, his father had a lot of problems. Problems Seth didn't need.

Robert shook his head. "I don't do drugs," he ground out.

"Just like you don't steal?" The words poured out of his mouth before Seth could stop them. "I noticed the missing money and your sudden birthday gift to Toby. All too coincidental, judging by the amount taken and the expensive gift."

A guilty expression instantly stole over his father's face. Seth wanted to be wrong, but Robert's reaction proved quite the opposite.

"I didn't steal the money. It was sitting there in a can, like an emergency fund. And discovering I missed my one and only grandson's birthday seemed like an emergency to me. I planned to pay it back," Robert snapped.

Seth shook his head. "Sure you did. I've had enough of your lies, and I want you off the ranch. *Today.*"

Robert seemed at a loss, his eyes glistening with unshed tears. "I belong here as much as you do," he said, desperation in his voice.

"Not the way I see it. And not the way Grandma and Grandpa saw it. So until there's a legal ruling on the document I suspect is fraudulent, I want you out of here. There's a bed and breakfast in town where I'm sure you can find a room." Seth hammered in the final nail on the exit sign. He fully expected his father to argue back, but instead, Robert's shoulders slumped, as if in defeat.

"Fine. I'll go."

Seth nodded. "Good."

Hopefully Toby hadn't overheard the conversation with Robert, and the sound of the train in motion gave Seth hope the kid was playing and not all that interested in adult conversation. "Toby, three minutes," he called out, before turning to head for the kitchen.

His son would be devastated when Seth broke the news about his grandfather leaving, but more than that, finding out his mother wouldn't be calling would be a double trauma. It was going to have to be a really good gift to offset the emotional pain. And worse, was the part Seth played in what was happening in Toby's life. Guilt kicked him in the gut, knowing his focus had been all wrong when he was at the law firm, and now Toby was paying the price for his mistakes. Something he was determined to fix. Second chances only worked if you put your heart and soul into the effort.

Seth pulled out his phone and called Leslie.

"Good morning, Seth. Is everything okay?" It was the same question Alicia asked, but with an entirely different motivation.

"Everything is fine," he lied. "I'm going to pick Toby up after school so I won't be needing you to bring him home."

"That's an excellent idea. He needs more one-on-one time with you."

"I hear you. Just wanted to make sure you knew the change in plans." Seth had no intentions of explaining what was happening, not if he didn't want another lecture from the schoolteacher on the saintliness of his father. But perhaps he did need to take a play out of Leslie's playbook and spend time trying to get closer to Toby in order to discover what he needed to do to make things right.

He could just ask Leslie, but that would mean admitting he was wrong, and she was right, or worse, that he needed her. And the problem was, he sensed he needed her for more than advice...his feelings growing for her as a person. Someone unlike anyone he'd ever met.

Being around her was like opening a can of sunshine. But life had taught him too much time in the sun and you get burned.

Seth had just enough time to get back to the ranch and meet the vet. Today was a big day...the biggest since they'd arrived from L.A. The morning hadn't gotten off to an auspicious start, but hopefully, the vet had good news. If both mares turned up pregnant, he and Toby would have a celebration. One that would make his son forget all about what was troubling him.

He pulled in and parked next to the old red Chevy. It would seem Dr. Walters had already arrived and was inside the barn. Seth headed in to join the vet. "Hey Fred, sorry I'm running a little late."

"You're fine. I used the time to talk to these sweet ladies and get them relaxed. Of course, the sugar cube most likely did all the work." Fred chuckled.

"That and carrots are their favorites."

"Shall I get started?" Fred asked.

"Absolutely. This is either going to be the best news ever, or the worst. I could barely sleep last night thinking about it."

"I understand. Breeding is an expensive venture and when you're just starting out, the anxiety can be off the charts. But look at it this way...each mare has a fifty-fifty shot." Fred picked up his medical bag and entered Genevieve's stall. "I'll start with her," he said, stopping to rub the horse's neck and mane, then moving down her side and brushing her flank. It was a calming process that worked well, the mare quietly allowing him to check her over.

Seth needed more like a hundred-hundred shot, but he didn't plan to get into his finances with the vet from Dallas. The doctor's fees alone had set Seth back a fortune, but he needed answers now, not in three or four months with an ultrasound. Only someone of Dr. Walters' caliber would have the ability to examine a mare and know for sure this early. "I'll hold her head and talk to her, to keep her occupied."

"Thanks." Fred went to work, the process taking quite some time. He murmured a few non-committal sounds, but otherwise, remained silent. Fred removed the gloves he'd used for the exam and tossed them in a trash bag. He closed up his medical bag and moved out of the stall.

Seth knew the answer before the vet said anything. *Not pregnant.* Otherwise, there would have been smiles and a jovial cheer before the man had finished the examination. A lump formed in his throat, making it difficult to swallow.

"Sorry, Seth. These things happen. Perhaps next time. And we still have Lady Jane," Fred said, trying to find a way to remain positive.

One horse would be better than none. He could start cutting back, perhaps convince Jarod at the bank to extend his line of credit based on future prospects. Something. "Let's hope," Seth said, unable to muster any enthusiasm. His and Toby's future were riding on today's results and he'd just gotten his first dose of bad news.

They repeated the process with Lady Jane, and by the time Fred was finished, an overwhelming sense of defeat had Seth's head spinning.

"I'm sorry, Seth. She's not pregnant either. It could be the stress of having just arrived here. There's a number of things that could happen, but the good news is they are healthy and will be adjusted during their next cycle. Keep the faith," Fred said, packing up his medical bag.

"Next time? I don't see how there can be a next time. I appreciate everything you have done, but for me, I think the breeding center doors have closed before they were even officially open."

"Surely, there's got to be another way, Seth. They are fine mares."

"Maybe so, but then, if I sell them it will go a long way to cover some of my loss." Seth was resigned to the truth and all his grand plans had failed.

"Well, if you change your mind, let me know," Fred said. They shook hands and the vet left.

Seth still couldn't believe neither mare had gotten pregnant. He'd started with two to even the odds, but it turned out, the odds were still against him. Come Monday, Seth would need to start looking for a real job. Maybe at one of the local law offices, or even the five and dime.

His father's words came back to haunt Seth.

Unemployed meant he would have to take any job he could if he expected to pay the bills. Any more credit against the ranch and he would risk losing everything...including the ranch. Which might happen anyway if Robert took it away. Life had dealt him another blow. When would God hear his prayers?

Seth rode out into the pastures, trying to understand the twists and turns of life, and failing. It was getting close to two by the time he returned, none the wiser or more reassured about the future. The only thing he did know was that he had failed Toby. The same as Alicia.

The grand plan this morning had been to stop at the store and get Toby a monster toy truck and a stuffed dog, then head for the park, and take in dinner and a movie. That was when he expected good news. Toby still deserved an outing, but Seth would trim back on the toys. Cutting expenses would be the way moving forward, but tonight, he wouldn't fall short on the outing plans. If anything, there was more reason to devote his time to Toby, something he intended to do every day.

Seth pulled into the pickup line and searched the sea of children's faces for his son. Toby wasn't with the group of kids standing near the assistant teacher. Maybe Leslie forgot or misunderstood that it was today that Seth planned to pick Toby up after school.

Seth turned the ignition off, slid out of the car and headed for Miss Coble. "Have you seen Toby? I let Leslie know I was picking him up today."

"He was just here. I went to help another child get buckled in, and when I came back, he was gone, so I figured you must have picked him up," she said, her voice fraught with worry.

Seth frowned. "Then he's got to be here, somewhere."

They both continued to search the waiting area, but as the children thinned out in numbers, there was still no sign of Toby.

Unease settled in the pit of Seth's stomach, concern mounting. "I'll go check the classroom. Perhaps he went back there for something. Or to see Miss Sullivan." Yes, that had to be it. Leslie.

"That's a great idea to check the classroom, but as for Leslie, she left not long ago."

"I see." Seth picked up his pace as he headed for the classroom, searching the halls for his son. His heart plummeted when he couldn't find him there, either. Seth returned to Susan, hoping she had more information.

"I looked in the classroom and around the school. Where can he be?" Seth asked, worry settling in deep.

"I don't know. Toby's got to be here somewhere. He just has to be. Let me call Principal Hill and her assistant, Miss Bradley, to see if they know anything. We need more people to search the school and they can organize it while I stay here with the rest of the children. I'm sorry," Susan said, her distress genuine.

Principal Hill joined them less than a minute later. "I'm sorry, Mr. Dillinger. I'm sure Toby is here and everything will be fine. This is a small town and everyone knows everyone. Susan, can you tell me what you remember?"

"We all went out to recess, but Toby didn't seem interested in playing today. He sat off to the side by himself and then came in with the other kids. The children all packed up their backpacks to go home. Leslie signed Toby out to allow him to join the kids in the pickup line, and he came outside with me. I went to help Sarah get in her mother's car and make sure she had her seatbelt on, and when I came back, Toby was gone. I figured his father picked him up and I missed it."

It was the same story she'd already recited to Seth, and he believed her. But it didn't help him find his son.

Susan started to cry.

"It's not your fault, Susan. Let's just stay calm and set up a more thorough search of the school for him," Principal Hill said, taking charge.

Seth was more than a little upset, but the truth was, the principal was right. Susan hadn't done anything wrong. Right now, however, all focus needed to be on finding Toby.

Principal Hill mentioned Crossroads Creek as a small town where everyone knew everyone. It was a comforting thought.

The image of an old, battered car with Colorado tags flashed in his head. His father wasn't local. And it stood to reason, Toby would leave with Robert without question. What if his father left the ranch, but took Toby with him? He didn't honestly believe his father would stoop that low...but Toby was missing.

If they couldn't find his son at school, Seth would check the ranch and call Sheriff Jones. "I'll head around the school to the right. And I'll call Leslie to see what she knows. Toby loves her and maybe he said something to her or she noticed something."

Principal Hill nodded. "I'll get some of the other teachers to search inside and I'll head around the school to the left. I'm sure we'll find him."

Seth prayed she was right because the alternative wasn't something he could handle.

What if something had happened to Toby? It was every parent's worst nightmare.

Worse than losing the ranch...would be losing Toby.

♥

Leslie finished picking out what she wanted for supper and headed for the checkout counter.

"Looks like someone's having chicken pot pie for dinner," Wanda said, a friendly smile at the ready. The elderly cashier had been working at the Super Saver for as long as Leslie could remember, and every day, she had a smile for all who came through her line.

"It would seem that way. But it's just for me. I find it handy to make a super-sized casserole and then freeze it into single-serving portions. My heat and eat meals." Leslie laughed. "Living alone, I've learned it works the best. Specially after a day at school when I'm ready to kick up my feet and relax and not spend hours in the kitchen for a good meal."

"Works for me too. But I do it for me and my husband. He's pretty easy to please when it comes to cooking." Wanda grinned. "That'll be $16.53 please."

Leslie swiped her debit card as Wanda bagged the groceries.

"You're all set. Have a good afternoon and a good dinner," Wanda said, handing her the grocery bags.

Leslie's phone rang. She slid the bags over one arm and pulled out her phone. "Thanks, Wanda," she called out as she headed for the door, trying to silence the ringer. The screen flashed Beth's name, alerting Leslie her best friend was calling. "What's up, Beth? I'm just finishing up at the store."

"What's for dinner?" It was a running joke between the two of them, practically inviting oneself to the other's house for dinner.

And with all the extra time she'd spent at the Dillinger ranch, they hadn't enjoyed any get-togethers lately. "Chicken pot pie if you're game?" Leslie said.

"I'd love to, but believe it or not, I've got a date tonight," Beth said, taking Leslie off guard.

"I don't believe it. Seriously, what are you up to?"

"I am being serious. I met a guy in Fontana at the coffee shop, and we agreed to have dinner. Just friends, but a change of pace."

"So much for the self-imposed dating ban," Leslie teased.

"Like I said, just friends. Something you could try with your cowboy. And if not your cowboy, find someone else."

Leslie put the groceries in the back seat of the car. "I'm happy for you. But trust me...I'm too busy for all the work that goes into a relationship." Beth in a relationship meant Leslie would get more pushes, or more like shoves, her friend always seeking the same happiness for her Leslie.

"Oh, you keep saying that, but I saw you at Toby's birthday party. I didn't miss all the little special looks you kept sending Seth. I think you should step up and let him know you're interested and to heck with the school rules. I mean, two people have to start somewhere and you could be very discreet. Just be friends...you know, do things together."

"For the last time, it's not going to happen. It's not just the school rules and you know it," Leslie reminded her friend. Not that they agreed on the issue, but it was Leslie's decision.

"I think you're using the parent rule as a way to avoid facing your feelings. I know you. Don't let your personal issues ruin what could be perfect. All it takes is that you're perfect for each other. And you won't know unless you show them you're interested and see what he says. It's not like I didn't see him checking you out."

Leslie heaved a heavy sigh. "Seth was grateful that I saved the day for him. That's all. A temporary condition. Trust me." Leslie started the car and headed for home.

"If it was a one-day temporary thing, then how come you ate dinner there the other evening?" Beth pressed the issue, zeroing in on the truth.

"Seth was looking for a buffer between him and his father, and I agreed to stay. It was nothing more than that and I was glad to help, considering I'm the one who set up the meal for the two of them to work through their issues. It was the least I could do. Although unfortunately it seems to have backfired." After she arrived home last night, she'd done some serious thinking about the situation, and was resigned to thinking Seth was right. She was a busybody, and it was time she butt out.

"So you're telling me you have zero interest in the cowboy?" Beth asked. "Truth time. Friendship honor."

Leslie would have liked to have kept silent but calling out the friendship honor card, there was no way to get around the issue. She did like

Seth. And she would have liked his kiss, she was sure of it. "Does it count if he kissed me?" she asked, wishing she could see her best friend's face. It was just a small case of pushing back, something to hold Beth in check.

"You don't say! Woohoo! And in case you don't know what that means, I'm doing a happy dance."

"Well, you can stop dancing. It was an in-the-moment thing. A moonlit night after we watched a kids' movie...truly just a blip on the radar."

"Oh, I think a kiss is way more than a blip on the radar. So how was it?" Beth asked, determined to get all the details.

"It's hard to say, because it didn't actually happen. I mean, he almost kissed me. But Toby interrupted us. It was for the best." Because for one temporary moment of insanity, she would have let him kiss her.

"I think it's interesting, and I think it shows potential. Like I've said a million times, you never know where life is going to take you. But if the opportunity presents itself, don't let life pass you by and keep you from finding out if there could be more between the two of you. Don't sell him short, Leslie."

Her phone rang, and she glanced at the screen and was surprised to see it was Seth. Why on earth would he be calling her when he was out having a good time with Toby? "I think Seth's ears were burning with all this talk about him. Let me call you right back, because he's calling in and I can't imagine what he wants."

"See what I mean? You drop everything for that man. I rest my case."

"More like case closed," Leslie said with a grin, disconnecting the call with Beth and pressing the connect button on the incoming caller as she pulled into the driveway. "Hey there, I didn't expect to hear from you this afternoon. Are you two having fun?"

"None. Toby's missing. I went to pick him up from school and he had simply vanished. They've searched Parkview Elementary and the surrounding area. I'm headed back to the ranch while Sheriff Jones and some of the other teachers continue to look around the school. They're getting some other folks to help start searching town as well."

Leslie's heart froze as Seth uttered each word, words she never wanted to hear about any child. "Oh no. I'm so sorry. Tell me what happened?" She tried to stay focused, fear for Toby threatening to overwhelm her.

"Just like I said...I went to pick him up, and he wasn't there. Susan Coble said she went to help another student and when she came back, he was gone. She assumed I'd picked him up and that somehow she'd missed him leaving. Except I had only just arrived. We've searched everywhere we could possibly think of," Seth said, desperation echoing in his voice.

Leslie tried to shove aside her fears and think. Keeping cool would do far more in this situation. "Has anyone called all the parents to see if the other kids might have seen something? Maybe someone gave him a ride to the ranch." It was a long shot, but every clue helped. They'd never had a child go missing and the community wouldn't rest until they'd checked everywhere.

"Talking to the kids was one of the things Sheriff Jones mentioned. He's getting a couple of his officers to tackle the job. I'm checking the ranch because of my father. I know you and I don't agree completely on him, but I've told the sheriff what I know, and he's on the lookout for my father as we speak."

Leslie dropped the groceries on the counter and started to put the food away. "Your father? I don't understand. What does he have to do with Toby missing?" Seth had gone too far this time. *Way too far.*

"This morning I had a confrontation with my father. It ended with me asking him to leave. And before you say anything, it's not just the money. I wasn't going to say anything like you suggested, but when he came out of the shower, everything changed. He had what looked like pinpoint holes in his arms around the veins. I think he's using drugs, although he denied it. There was no way I could let him stay, but now I'm worried if he would retaliate and take Toby as a way to punish me." Seth opening up to her with his deepest fears, spoke volumes about the depth of his feeling for his son and his state of worry.

Leslie pushed aside her own worry for the child, knowing worry wouldn't help find him...action would. "Robert loves Toby, and he wouldn't hurt his grandson. And I don't believe for a minute he's using drugs. You need to approach this from an outside point of view. He doesn't come in acting high or strange. There's other reasons people get injections, and as your father, you should give him the benefit of the doubt."

"Then where is he?" Seth asked quietly. Almost too quiet.

An image of Toby sitting in class flashed across her mind. He seemed out of sorts all day, and although she'd asked him on more than one occasion, he denied being upset about anything. Now she wondered if she should have pressed him harder and not ignored the signs. "I was just thinking Toby didn't seem himself today. Is it possible he overheard you talking with your dad this morning? That couldn't have been a pleasant conversation."

"I suppose anything is possible, but highly doubtful. He was in his room getting ready for school and the train set was running. And just because I had a discussion with my dad doesn't mean it was a shouting one. And I'm pretty sure his door was closed."

"Okay. I'm just trying to figure out why he was so upset today. It's not like him shutting me out. Maybe he had an altercation with a kid at school. I wish I had talked to him more," Leslie offered. She prided herself on being there for the kids and had let Toby down by the looks of things.

"Me too. I had a fun afternoon planned for him and was even going to pick him up a couple of new toys I know he would love, although that part of the plan changed. I'm trying, Leslie, but I'm beginning to think I'll never get the parenting thing right."

Leslie shook her head. Seth hadn't heard a word she said before about trying to buy a kid's affection. It simply didn't work that way, at least not long term. And parenting was a long-term gig. "That's a discussion for another time, but you can't buy his love. Spending time with him, now that was the right decision."

"I'm at the ranch now and need to go look for Toby."

"Okay. He couldn't have gotten too far. I just got into the house myself. Give me five minutes and I'll head back to the school to meet you there when you finish checking the ranch. We'll find him. We have to," Leslie said, wanting to reassure Seth, even though she had no way of knowing the outcome. But she was determined not to give in to the fear and let it control her...or Seth if she could help it. What she could control was her prayers and the hope Toby would be found.

"Sounds good. Thanks. Oh, and Leslie...I'm about to figure out if your faith in my father is well placed, because although I ordered him off the ranch, his car is still here."

"Talk to him, Seth. I'm sure he'll be just as upset as you are with Toby's disappearance. I'll see you shortly. Make sure you call me if you hear anything or find him."

Leslie hung up the phone and tossed the entire bag of groceries into the refrigerator. She'd sort them out later, but right now she needed to let Jelly outside for a quick potty break. Every minute counted, and she wanted to be in on the search for Toby.

"Jelly," Leslie called out. The dog always greeted her at the door, so she was surprised not to find him underfoot. "Come on, girl, we need to make this quick. Mommy's got to run and help find Toby." *Poor kid.* What if he simply wandered off and was lost? Crossroads Creek was a small town and Leslie wasn't willing to go the dreaded route of something more sinister at work. *Not yet anyway.*

"Jelly? Where are you?"

The dog barked from one of the back bedrooms. Leslie made her way down the hall, wondering if she'd somehow got locked in. "Jelly, come on. There isn't time to play hide and go seek."

She entered the room, but the dog was nowhere to be seen. As Leslie moved to investigate, she rounded the bed and spotted Jelly's tail thumping on the carpet, though the rest of her was hidden under the bed. "Come on, girl. Did you find something? Hopefully nothing furry because you know I can't stand mice in the house." Leslie kneeled, preparing herself for the worst, as the dog hadn't moved.

Except what she saw moved her to tears.

Toby.

The rush of relief overwhelmed her and it took a few seconds to speak. "What are you doing here, sweetie?" she asked softly, not wanting to scare him. His tear-streaked face was almost her undoing.

He sniffed. "I came to see Jelly," Toby said, reaching out to pet the dog as though drawing comfort from her.

"I'm so glad you're okay. We can talk about this in a minute, but first I need to call your dad. He's worried sick about you."

"My mom's not. She doesn't even want me," Toby choked out the words as he sniffed.

"I'm sure that's not true. Will you trust me and come out from under the bed so we can talk about this? Please," Leslie urged, holding out her hand.

Toby shook his head. "I want to stay here. With you. Please don't make me leave."

Leslie was at a loss for what to say. "I'll be right back and we can talk about this." And it would give her a moment to figure out what to say.

Once out in the hall, she hit redial to call Seth.

"What's up? I just talked—"

"He's here, Seth. Toby's here. At my house." Tears streamed down her face, the rush of emotion running unchecked now that Toby couldn't see her.

"Your house? Thank the Lord. But your house? I don't understand. And how did he get there? And why is he there?" Seth fired off the questions, his voice breaking with emotion.

Leslie's heart went out to Seth. So many unanswered questions, and somehow, Leslie was deeply involved. Something Seth wouldn't appreciate. "I don't know yet. He's staying put under the bed and I need to go back and talk to him. I just wanted to tell you that he is here and that he's okay."

"Thank you, Leslie. I'll let everyone know and I'll be at your place soon. Please, don't let him out of your sight," Seth said in a rush. "I can't lose him again."

"You have my word. I'll see you in a few minutes. Oh, and I live at 45 Candy Cane Lane. Just south of the town limits, first drive to the right.

It's a small blue cottage with white shutters and a huge front porch. You can't miss it."

"Gotcha. I'm on my way."

Leslie hung up and moved back into the bedroom. She lay down on the floor, as close as she could to the underside of the bed. She gave Jelly a pat on the back. "Good girl." The dog thumped her tail in response. She was a small dog, but a good protector. And probably a good listener as well.

"Toby, I'm here for as long as you need me, but we do have to talk. And this conversation might be easier if we were sitting together." She patted the floor next to where she lay.

"Okay," he said, scooting forward. She wrapped her arms around him, her squeeze more like a bear hug. Something they both needed.

"Thank you," she said, placing a kiss on the top of his head. "Let's sit right here and talk about this. You can tell me anything and I will do everything in my power to help. I promise," Leslie wanted to reassure him, but the truth was, she would do everything within her power. Which ultimately wasn't much. Seth would be the one to work through the issue with his son.

"My mom and dad were arguing this morning about me. I heard my dad's raised voice, and I cracked open the door to hear. He never gets mad like he was this morning," Toby said.

This was the first Leslie had heard about Seth calling Toby's mother. "Eavesdropping never brings good results, but I understand your curiosity. Go on," she prompted him to continue.

"I told my dad I was upset because my mom never even calls me. I reckon he called her and then they got mad at each other again and it's all my fault. Mine and her stupid new husband. My mom got married and didn't even tell me," Toby said, tears running down his cheeks as he sobbed out the words.

"Please don't call people stupid. It's okay to be upset by the news, but it doesn't make anyone stupid. I'm sure he's a very nice man if she married him." At the very least, two people suited for each other. And based on what little

Leslie knew, Toby was better off without the selfish woman playing with his emotions.

Toby shook his head. "And she's gonna have a baby. She doesn't need me anymore. That's why she doesn't call me."

"I'm sure that's not true. You're a very special young man and perhaps your mother is super busy with her new life. Just like you're super busy in your new life making friends, going to school, and next week, you start in with your riding lessons." Leslie didn't want to make excuses for the woman, but this was about far more than Seth's ex-wife. This was about Toby.

All of it.

"I guess," he shrugged. "It's just not fair. And just when I found out I have a grandpa who loves me, my dad made him leave. I want to live with you. You have a pretty house, not like ours. And you can cook. And then there's Jelly," Toby said, listing out his reasons and hoping it would make a difference.

"But honey, what about your dad? He loves you so much and he would be broken-hearted if you didn't live with him. And as to the house, it's just a matter of time before your dad has it all fixed up. And I'm sure you'll get a dog at some point. And as for your grandpa, give it time. Adults can be a little slow to forgive, but eventually they come around." Or at least Leslie hoped they would.

"Naw. Dad just works all the time. It's what my mother always used to say, and she was right. He doesn't have time for me," Toby said, sounding far older and wiser than his seven years.

"I'm sure if you talked to him and told him how you feel, things could be different. Or I could talk to him for you if you'd like," Leslie offered, grasping at straws, and trying to figure out what to say to change his mind.

Toby looked up at her, a sudden light in his eyes. "Would you? Do you think it would help?"

"We can try." She gave him another hug. "But Toby, don't ever run off like this again. You had everyone worried sick. How did you get here, anyway?"

"In your car. I snuck in before you left school and hid when you came here. I was scared when you left because I've never been alone, but I figured I would be brave like Jelly. She's always home alone during the day when you are at school." Toby wiped his shirt on his cheeks to dry his face.

"I was just getting ready to go help your dad, the sheriff, and everyone in town look for you, so I'm glad Jelly let me know you were here."

"The sheriff and other people?" Toby suddenly looked frightened. "Am I going to jail?"

"No silly. They were looking for you because they love you and didn't want anything to happen to you. Running off was wrong, but your punishment, I'm quite sure will be big hugs. Your safety is most important. And although you have your reasons for running off and being upset, you need to remember to talk to adults. I'm always here if you need me." Seth might not like her interference, but Toby needed to know he had a friend. No matter what.

Leslie was glad Toby hadn't pressed harder on the subject of living here. More to the point, she was sure what Toby really wanted was a mother to replace the one he felt was lost. Which made it all the harder to tell him no, considering it was the same thing she wanted. Sort of. Not a mother, but a child.

And Toby...she would love him to pieces if he were her own.

Chapter Seventeen

♥

AFTER ALERTING EVERYONE THAT Toby was safe, Seth had raced to Leslie's house, slowing only to make sure he followed her directions correctly. The overwhelming fear that had gripped him had subsided, but the need to hold his son in his arms had grown.

When no one had answered the door, he had let himself in. It had been the sound of Leslie's and Toby's voices down the hall that caught his attention. But what he heard had caused him to stop and listen.

As the two talked, Toby's words ripped Seth's heart to pieces. His son had run off because of him. The call to Alicia. His falling out with his dad and ordering him off the property. When would Seth learn? Just when he thought he might have parenting figured out, he was dealt a blow.

But this time, he would do better. There was no other choice. Toby came first...in everything. Somewhere along the line, the parenting factor had kicked into gear. He would have another chance to be the father he should have been all along.

The two of them were a team.

"I love you, Miss Sullivan," Toby declared, a depth of emotion in his son's voice he hadn't heard in a long time. But the words should have been said to his father...not his teacher.

"I love you, too. Now dry your eyes. Your dad should be here soon. Let's show him your brave face and then we'll talk more."

Seth started forward, not wanting to be caught eavesdropping, and needing to put an end to the conversation before his son was confused more than he already was.

"Okay. I'll be brave...for you."

"Toby," Seth said, holding out his arms. It came with great relief when his son jumped up and raced towards him. Proof it wasn't too late to fix everything if Toby's reaction was anything to go by. "I love you." He kneeled, coming level with his son, needing to be close and see for himself that he was fine.

"I love you too, Dad. And I'm sorry if I worried you," Toby said, glancing up at his teacher as if for approval.

Seth couldn't help the surge of jealousy he felt toward Leslie. "I'm just glad you're okay." He hugged his son tightly, wanting to never let him go.

"Miss Sullivan took good care of me. So did Jelly." Toby grinned.

"You and I need to talk. Perhaps we should say goodbye to Miss Sullivan and let her enjoy the rest of her day. Thank you so much, Leslie. I'm grateful he had the foresight to make his run with you, although I much prefer to avoid all of this in the future."

"You're welcome. And I totally agree. We should talk about this. Maybe if you want to give me a call later," Leslie said.

Except Seth knew what she wanted to tell him, and he didn't need her help. Not this time. He had more than enough information to know what to do. And by the sound of things, it was high time to cut short the extra time Toby's teacher hung around the ranch. For his son's sake. "I'll talk to Toby and if I feel the need, I'll give you a call," Seth snapped, unable to take much more.

Leslie pulled back in shock and frowned. "We really—"

Maybe he could have said it better, but she didn't know he had heard most of their conversation and was well-informed. Or that he was at the end of his ropes and needed to regroup. Before he fell apart in front of Toby. Or her. "Again, thanks for taking such good care of him. Toby and I have some talking to do, so we best be on our way." Seth turned and walked down the hall and out the door.

Toby climbed in the back seat and buckled his seat belt as Seth slid into the driver's seat.

"Dad, why did you send Grandpa away? I liked having him at the ranch." Toby was getting straight to the point, which was probably a good thing, but it also hadn't left Seth much time to prepare.

He glanced in the rearview mirror as he pulled away from the cottage. "We just don't agree on some things. I was upset about some things and perhaps acted in haste." Innocent until proven guilty, but Seth hadn't allowed that to affect his decision. Besides, his dad did help himself to the household emergency funds.

"You always tell me not to say anything when I'm mad cause it's never going to be good. And you tell me I need to be forgiving. Maybe grandpa didn't mean to make you mad."

Toby didn't understand, but then he shouldn't. It was adult business. "That's true. I should heed my own advice. Thanks for the reminder, son." *Forgiveness*. It's what was preached last Sunday at church, but wasn't there a limit? Pastor Phil's words echoed in his head. Forgiveness allows you to move on and embrace joy in your own life...not letting anger or hurt control you. It was freeing to the person who gave it.

It made more sense now than Seth wanted to admit, but it was true. His father had taken the money, yes, but he used it for Toby. To bring joy. And it's not like Seth couldn't afford it. Or couldn't afford until today, that is. And it was his father. A man not deserving of forgiveness. But then, the past had held Seth hostage for so long...perhaps it was time to let go.

"Is that the only thing that upset you?" Seth asked, already knowing there was more, but wanting to clear the air.

Toby shook his head. "I heard you talking to mom. She doesn't love me, does she?"

"I'm sorry I called her when you were nearby. That's on me. But as for your mother not loving you, why would you think that?" Seth couldn't recall those words ever being used in the conversation.

"Because she's married to someone else and having a baby."

Seth let out a deep breath. "Your mother is busy with her new life. I'm sure she still loves you in her own way, but she's got more people to consider and take care of. And don't forget, she knows you have me. And I promise you, from here on out, we are going to make a great team. But I need you to talk to me when you're upset. Otherwise, I can't help fix things."

"Okay, Dad. Since mom's married, maybe you could marry someone else too. Someone like Miss Sullivan. She would make a great mom," Toby said.

Seth was startled by the suggestion, although he shouldn't have been. It was only a matter of time before his son started feeling the need for a mom to replace the one who didn't have time for him. How anyone could walk away the way Alicia did was beyond Seth, but it didn't mean he had to replace her. Explaining that to

Toby in a way he would understand wouldn't be easy. "There's more to marriage than being a mother."

He pulled into the driveway and spotted Robert's car still parked out front. Seth's order for him to leave had taken a backseat to Toby's disappearance, his father equally concerned for his grandson.

Now, Seth was reminded of the promise he'd made to Robert before he left for Leslie's. The promise for a face-to-face discussion. A real honest-to-goodness discussion about the past and the future. It was time to sort out the mess they'd made, if for no other reason than Toby. That in itself was reason enough for Seth to step out of his comfort zone.

"Toby am I ever glad to see you," Robert said, rushing to his grandson's side and kneeling to take him in a bear hug.

There was genuine pleasure in the old man's face, something Leslie seemed to have noticed well before Seth.

"Thanks, Grandpa. And I'm super happy to see you too. Please don't leave," Toby said, glancing up at Seth, as if to make sure it was okay he'd said what he did.

Seth nodded to give his son reassurance. Toby wouldn't be caught up in an adult affair anymore if he could help it. "Toby, I need to talk to your grandfather for a minute. Any chance you'd like to play with your train set?" Seth prompted.

"Oh yes, I forgot about them. Thanks again Grandpa for the awesome birthday present. I love my new bedroom," Toby said, heading into the house without so much as a backward glance.

The minute Toby left, Robert's expression changed. His father seemed much older...tired, his expression almost one of defeat. An expression Seth put there by turning him out from his home.

They moved to sit on the porch.

"Thanks for agreeing to talk to me," Robert said.

Seth was at a loss for how to answer, especially given the news he'd gotten this morning. It changed everything, but where to begin, Seth didn't have a clue. "No problem."

Robert rocked in the chair at a steady pace, gazing out at the countryside. "After our, *ummm*, discussion this morning, I left here and went to see my doctor."

Seth frowned. "Doctor? I didn't know you had a doctor here in town."

"There's a lot you don't know, but I aim to fix that right here and now. I can't do this anymore," Robert said, his voice low enough Seth had to lean in to catch the words.

"Do what?" he asked.

"Avoid the truth," Robert said, turning to face Seth.

"What—"

Robert held up his hand. "Let me just say all that I need to say, and then you can say what you want, throw me out again, or anything else you come up with, as I probably deserve it all. Or worse, for everything I've done."

Seth nodded, especially given he didn't know what to say based on a prelude to a conversation with such intensity.

"First, let me say I'm sorry about leaving when you were eight. Marriage is a two-way street, and I took a turn on a one-way street with a dead end. I can't change the past, but I do regret it and I'm sorry."

Seth wanted to jump in and say a thing or two. *Forgiveness.* The word popped into his head again, helping him to stay focused...and quiet.

Robert stood and moved to the porch rail, holding on as if for support.

His father suddenly seemed old and frail.

"My doctor seems to think I haven't handled this trip home very well, and it's taking its toll on me in many ways. You see, I've got diabetes. Type 2 and it's advanced. I've also got kidney disease and the marks you see on my arms are from the dialysis treatments I receive at a facility in Dallas."

Seth cringed, knowing what he'd said and suspected. Did Leslie have to be right about everything? Or was it simply a matter of her seeing things from a more positive aspect? Believing in the good of people. "Sorry to hear that, and about what I said," Seth interjected, wanting to clear the air.

"Thank you. But there's more, and lots you won't like. Stuff I'm ashamed to admit, but a man can only do so much before life sets him straight about what's important in his life."

"Go on," Seth said, realizing he too had just come face to face with the same lesson. Perhaps they did have more in common they he cared to admit.

"It was a combination of diabetes and continued poor health choices for diet and a sedentary lifestyle that eventually led to kidney disease. Daily insulin shots and dialysis treatments are a way of life for me now."

"I had no idea," Seth said, shaking his head.

"You wouldn't know because I hadn't told you. Truth is, I came to the ranch because I can't afford the treatments and housing. So I showed up here, hoping the place was deserted.

It was my home once upon a time and it was the only place left I knew I could come to."

Seth frowned, quickly putting two and two together and not liking what it added up to. "And the will?"

Robert rubbed at his temples and let out a deep sigh. "I'm so sorry. It's a fake. When I arrived, the plan was to file the paperwork and take over the deserted ranch since it seemed you weren't interested. But then it turned out you were living here with Toby, something I hadn't expected. Heck, I didn't know I had a grandson, but that's my own fault."

"So why not just tell me the truth?" Seth asked, blown away by the admission. Not to mention, relieved.

"I didn't have much choice, as you would have thrown me out instantly if I didn't give you a reason to let me stay. I know you hate me for the past, but I'm tired of running and never finding a home. I won't win any father of the year award, but I'm trying to make a difference now. I'd like to be there for Toby, and you, if you can steer your way clear to giving me a chance."

Seth shook his head, his father's words sinking in. "You were going to try to steal the place from me and your grandson?" This was like fresh salt on an old wound ripped open.

"Not my best idea. I'm sorry. I always knew you would figure it out anyway and that my days here were limited, but truly, I needed a place to rest. It about killed me when the folks disinherited me, but I reckon I see their point of view now that I'm older. And they did leave it to my son, so it stayed in the family. Glad you never sold it."

"So am I." Seth nodded, acknowledging the truth in his own heart. *Forgiveness.* His father wasn't perfect, but then, neither was Seth. "I've not always done things right in my life, either. Mistakes are made when people are young and dumb. I, for one, am grateful for the opportunity for a do-over with Toby. I reckon I should give you the same chance."

Robert's face brightened considerably. "Thank you. It's more than I could hope for. But there is one more thing."

"What's that?" Seth asked. He was already taking a giant leap forward with faith in letting his father stay at the ranch and get to know his grandson. What else could Robert possibly want?

"I'm hoping you'll give me a chance...with you," his father said, looking him dead in the eye and not backing down.

This was something Seth hadn't considered. Wasn't sure he could. "I don't know. A lot's happened. We can take it one day at a time. You can make the bunkhouse your home, and health permitting, maybe help me out at the ranch here and there, but there's something you should know." If his dad was being honest, Seth needed to do the same.

"Oh, what's that?"

"Neither one of the mares are pregnant. The equine breeding center is a failure and there's no money to go another round. The business is a bust before it ever got started. I'll be looking for work in town, and you might need to do the same."

"I'm sorry. I know you had your heart set on this, but why can't you try again? Horse breeding is never a sure thing. Your grandmother and grandfather built this place into a success, and the very name should carry weight moving forward. You just need more horses. You can't give up now."

"Except I'm not willing to risk the ranch to make a go of it. I took out a credit line for the first vet expenses, Jarod, the loan officer at the bank said I'd have to put up the ranch as collateral for more money. I'm not willing to do that. I've worked sunup to sundown since I've been here and have nothing to show for it except a load of debt to repay."

"That's not true. You been working hard on the ranch and it shows. It's not just the horses, it's the homestead. I think you should try again," his father countered, surprising Seth with the compliment and the encouragement.

Unfortunately, the words didn't change anything. "My good looks won't get us twenty thousand dollars for the expenses. I've got to move on," Seth said.

"Maybe not. What about me? You've got me."

"Your good looks? I'm afraid that won't fly either. It takes cold, hard cash."

"Something you have if you mortgage the ranch. Combined with what I know about running the breeding center and all the ins and outs of the business, *we* could make it work. A team. I believe in you and I believe in what my parents built. I'd hate to see it fade into history."

Seth was shocked, the idea one that had never crossed his mind. His father had worked at the ranch until he walked away. "You really think we could make a go of this? The thought of losing the place doesn't sit well."

"There's always risk, but anything worth having, is worth going after with all your heart and soul. Your grandparents taught me everything I know, and trust me, there's a lot of ins and outs that can make this operation less expensive to run, and therefore, more successful. Not to mention, special treatments that help the mares become more fertile during the process. What do you say, Seth? You and me working together to make this happen," Robert said.

"It's a big decision, but perhaps you're the miracle the ranch needed. Yes, let's do this. Together," Seth said, before he thought about it for too long and talked himself out of the deal. Ever since he arrived here, he wanted the ranch restored to its former glory. And it would seem there was still hope...more than hope...a heavenly miracle.

Robert smiled and offered his hand, the two shaking to seal the deal. *Father and son.*

Seth had thought he lost everything today. Instead, it would seem he gained everything. A loving relationship with his son. A father. A partner. And with any luck, the equine center.

No, not luck. Seth had wondered why God never answered his prayers and he finally understood. He hadn't been ready...in his heart.

"Oh, and one other small ask," Robert said.

"Pushing your luck, huh?" Seth grinned, already feeling a load of pressure off his shoulders.

"Maybe. But can I pick Toby up after school each day to spend more time with him? I mean Leslie's super nice and all, but I figure I'm the one who should be watching him. My energy levels are lower in the afternoon, but I can give you a few hours work in the mornings and then take it easy with my grandson."

It was a *big* ask, considering he really didn't know or understand his father's medical issues. *Yet.* "I'll think about it. Right now, it's all worked out with Leslie until Toby's nanny returns. And I reckon they cook better than you." Seth shot Robert a grin to take the sting out of the rejection. Or it had been worked out. Now, Seth wasn't so sure the previous arrangement would work.

"Thanks Seth. It's all I can ask at this point."

"So, how is your health other than what you've said?" The question had been at the tip of his tongue since he found out his father was sick. The thought of losing him all over again didn't settle well.

"The doctors are doing all they can, and so far the treatments are working. I reckon my life is in God's hands at this point."

Seth hadn't taken his dad as a religious person, given at dinner not long ago he said as much. The sentiment came as a welcome surprise as he too had some recent revelations on the subject. "We probably shouldn't tell Toby anything about your health at this point, but I'm glad things are okay. Truly." He meant every word, and it felt good to say them out loud. At some point, he'd consider calling his mother to give her the head's up Robert was back in town. But for now, he'd let things lie and see how it all panned out.

"I agree. And thanks. I think I'll go pay Toby a visit and tell him the good news," Robert said, moving to the front door and disappearing inside.

Seth, on the other hand, needed to update Leslie and set her straight. It would be best if she didn't take care of Toby after school any longer but finding someone else he could trust until Claudia returned wouldn't be easy. His son was already pushing him toward Leslie, wanting a new mother, and it was up to Seth to put a stop to it. And even if he did want to get remarried, it wouldn't be for a mother to his son. He'd made the wrong choices before based on what he wanted out of life and wouldn't be making a repeat of history with more bad decisions based on a desired outcome.

It would have to be love, a love like his grandfather and grandmother shared. And maybe, just maybe, the answer regarding Toby's after school care was staring Seth right in the face. *His father.*

Who knows, maybe his dad had learned to cook along the way. If not, Seth would be relegated to the job.

It might not be good, but he was willing to learn for Toby's sake.

Chapter Eighteen

♥

LESLIE HOPED ALL HAD gone well with Toby and his father. She wanted to explain what Toby had shared with her, but the man reacted like he didn't care or didn't want to know. Except Leslie knew better. So why then did Seth act like he couldn't get out of her house fast enough and was determined to handle the issue on his own? Except she knew things, important things...information Seth needed.

After finishing her Chicken pot pie supper, freezing the extras, and cleaning the dishes, Leslie settled in her favorite plush recliner in the corner of the living room, hoping to get in some reading. She didn't find many free minutes to allow herself the luxury and intended to take full advantage.

The grandfather clock on the wall kept ticking the minutes away, but Leslie had yet to turn a single page. What she wanted was for Seth to call, but given his earlier attitude, it might be the calling would be left up to her. Afterall, it was in Toby's best interest.

This had nothing to do with the handsome cowboy who almost kissed her. A scene she had replayed over and over, trying to imagine what it would have been like. Leslie feared more than a little bit that her adamant denial of feelings toward the man would have been proven false. She liked his determination to succeed. Liked his fierce can-do attitude and the obvious love for his son, even if a bit unorthodox in showing it. Gifts were never the answer.

A kiss, however, might have proven she liked-liked Seth...something she was loath to admit as it would only lull her into a false sense of hope toward the man.

Leslie glanced at the phone on the end table next to her, wishing it would ring. The phone lit up, the incoming call tone ringing loud in the quiet living room. It was almost a little too uncanny, more so when she glanced at the screen.

Seth Dillinger.

"Hi, Seth. Is everything okay with Toby?" she asked, quickly covering what she considered most important in light of what they had all been through today.

"Toby's fine. I wanted to thank you again for taking good care of him until I got to your place," Seth said, an odd tone to his voice. *Business-like.*

"You're welcome. Have you called then to discuss what happened? Toby and I had a pretty enlightening conversation, and I feel it's important for you to know what he told me."

"I was in the hall and heard most of it, so no need to rehash."

She hadn't known Seth had been eavesdropping, but then, it was his son and he could do what he wanted. Toby's comments would not have been well received by his father and it explained Seth's gruff attitude earlier. "Then why are you calling?"

"I wanted to let you know I no longer need your after-school services," Seth said, cutting straight to the point.

A point she didn't understand. "You're firing me? I didn't do anything wrong. I didn't know he had hidden in my car." Not having time with Toby after school also meant her evenings spent as a family were over. Evenings she'd come to look forward to with great peace.

"It's not a firing, per se. Maybe I should have explained first. I'm not good expressing my feelings with words," Seth said, his tone much kinder.

"I'm listening," Leslie said, still in shock at the outcome.

"You were right about my father. Those marks on his arms are from dialysis treatments that he gets from an out-of-town doctor. It explains Robert's frequent absences from the ranch. He's also on daily insulin shots. His health isn't good, but it's stable right now. He needs a place to stay and wants to help out when he can, including taking care of Toby after school."

This wasn't anything she expected, and it made perfect sense. Except it didn't ease the feeling of loss. "I'm sorry to hear about his health. Toby will love spending more time with your father." More surprising was the fact it sounded like Seth and his father had come to some sort of agreement, something that would be good for all the Dillinger men.

"That's what I finally decided. Neither of the mares are pregnant and I was going to give up on the idea of the equine breeding center, but unbelievably, my dad and I are going to work on turning the business around...together. He's far more experienced and worked with my grandfather for years. It will be a partnership of sorts."

Leslie knew how important it had been to Seth, and how much he had been banking on success. "That's wonderful news. I mean, not about the mares...but about you and your father."

"Thank you. *Ummm*...there is one more thing," Seth said, his hesitation garnering her full attention.

"What's that?"

"This is the tricky part. You see, Toby loves you and there's no easy way to clue you in to what's going on, other than shooting straight. Toby has ideas about us getting married so that you can be his mother, something I can't do. I've tried to explain it to him, but I was hoping you might help me by paying less attention to Toby. I mean, oh, I don't know what I mean. Just don't encourage the boy. I'm not looking to get married again and anything in between would only confuse Toby more. I'm more of a loner and need to handle my family affairs on my own. It's less complicated this way."

The words *mother* and *married* echoed in her head. All things Leslie wanted, but with the right man. And to hear Seth summarily dismiss the idea, like marrying her was the last thing on earth he would want to do...hurt. "I understand and agree," she said, more stiffly than intended. "Not only that, but I don't date student's parents, so it's out of the question. Perhaps you could tell Toby about the school rules to help him understand and accept the situation."

Leslie was letting Seth off the hook, especially given that he had almost kissed her. *Talk about giving out the wrong signals.*

"Okay, then. I'll pass along that information. Thanks again for everything. And Leslie..."

Seth paused and she waited a few seconds for him to finish. "Yes?" she asked, at last when he said nothing else.

"Never mind. I was just thinking about something, but it doesn't matter," he said succinctly. "I've got to run, but I'm glad we talked and are on the same page."

"Yes. Have a good night." Leslie hung up the phone, clutching it to her chest. Toby wanted her as his mother, a role she would have loved.

The kid had touched her heart more deeply than she'd imagined and there was no greater compliment to be had. Even his cowboy father had wormed his way into her heart, and though she told him otherwise, his flat rejection left her reeling.

They weren't her family, even if deep down she had wanted that very thing. Leslie couldn't make Seth love her, though her own feelings had grown stronger with each passing day.

But she was really happy Seth and his father were trying to make things work. For Toby's sake, it was best.

Chapter Nineteen

♥

SETH REINED THE HORSE to the left with a slight nudge and headed for the house. The sun was setting, but the countryside view and serenity of the moment kept him out on the trail longer than he had planned. Mostly because he had a lot of thinking to do, something he did best on the back of his horse, combined with fresh air and sunshine.

The last few weeks of hard work may have gotten a lot done on the house but did little to rid Seth of the feeling of discontent that had settled deep in the pit of his stomach. Not even the news that, not one, but both mares had gotten pregnant the second time around had eradicated the sense of loss. The vet's news had been the miracle they needed. The ranch would be safe, and their future solidified. And then there was his father. The two of them had established a relatively peaceful existence, one that centered around the future and not the past...and they were doing well. And Toby, for sure, was happier. He had new friends and new family.

Which is why Seth was at a loss to understand the discontent. If the problem wasn't his dad, Toby, the house, or the ranch, there was only one obvious choice remaining. *Leslie.* She had managed to break down the wall around his heart and he could no longer deny the truth...he cared about her. Deeply. And not just as a nanny for his son.

Cared for her the way a man cares for the special lady in his life. Leslie was more than special...she was the epitome of perfect...perfect for him, that is. It did no good to deny his feelings knowing they had both been present the night he almost kissed her, and neither one of them would have ended the moment if Toby hadn't interrupted.

Early after Seth had arrived in Crossroads Creek, he hadn't been sure he even wanted to stay. And yet, he had changed his mind. Seth had never wanted anything to do with his dad again. And yet, he had changed his mind. And he wasn't interested in a relationship. And yet, it would seem that too might have changed.

Leslie was a part of Crossroads Creek. One of the best parts, if he was honest. She'd invaded his life, all to help. Although it had taken some doing to bring him around to see things her way...she had managed it quite well.

Did she get as involved with everyone or just him?

Because now, without her coming around, things were different and not in a good way. Seth missed her special touches all around the house. Flowers. Home-cooked meals. Toby's craft projects displayed on the mantle proudly, or his drawings on the refrigerator.

The house was clean and organized...but it felt flat and empty.

Not even bringing Claudia back to cook meals and help when his dad had doctor's visits quelled the longing for Leslie's bright and cheery face around the house. And there was only one reason she would have this kind of impact on him. It was time to face the truth.

He loved her. Seth hadn't gone looking for love, but somewhere between her busybody methods and honesty, he had fallen for her sweet loving personality and sunshine spirit. Coming back to Crossroads Creek and reconnecting with his past had been the best thing for him and Toby. But Seth had also managed to reconnect with his heart...something he'd thought was lost a long time ago.

And if coming home had given him a do over in life, the same held true for his heart. And Leslie was the key to change when it came to the affairs of his heart. It was a chance to get love right...for the first time in his life.

The more he thought about Leslie, and the more he embraced the truth, letting it sink in, the more it all became clear to him. If Seth asked her back into his life, he was sure she would think it was because of Toby. She would latch on to the idea Seth wanted a mother for his son. And yes, it was a bonus, but not the truth. He wanted Leslie in his life because life without her wasn't as bright or joyful. Coming home each night after a hard day of work had become his favorite part of the day. Without her there, things just weren't the same.

Leslie deserved the best from him and if he had any chance of convincing her of his true feelings, he would need to find a way to prove his love was for her and not what she could do for him.

The sun was setting and Seth needed to get back to the house. As he rode home, bits and pieces of conversations with Leslie flitted through his brain. And by the time he was home, he had a game plan in place.

Operation win Leslie's heart.

The week passed slowly, Seth eager for his plans to come to fruition. And not because he was finally taking a day off, but because of what was in store for the children. Not to mention his hope to show Leslie he understood what she had been trying to show him. Slow down life enough to enjoy the moment, not letting the joy of each day pass him by in search of what he only dreamed he wanted. Reality was so much better.

Susan Coble had done an amazing job of getting Principal Hill's permission first and then getting the signed permission slips from the parents. Leslie had been kept out of the loop intentionally. As far as she knew, they were going to the science center in Austin.

Far from it, but she would find out soon enough. Of course Susan had been all too happy to help Seth, the woman sensing romance was in the air. And she was right.

He stood off to one side as the bus parked. Everything was in place. The tables and chairs, the BBQ banquet, and of course, the Bouncy's R' Us inflatable slide and ball house.

The idea had come to Seth that he needed to show Leslie how he didn't always stand on the sidelines waiting for life to happen. A way to prove to Leslie he had changed and that he could get personally involved. With Toby. His father. The community. And with any luck...Leslie.

He spotted her as she stepped off the bus, looking around in confusion. Susan stood next to her and pointed in his direction.

Seth waved, moving toward her. "Good morning, Leslie. It looks like a great day for a field trip." He grinned.

"It does at that, but I'm a bit confused, seeing as I thought we were going to the science center. Susan told me to ask you about the change in itinerary as she had to see to the children. She's acting a little strange if you ask me and I think she's up to something. But what are you doing here? Are you a chaperone?"

"You could say that," Seth teased, shooting her a wink. All in good time, she'd find out the whole truth. Actions spoke louder than words and today, he was a man of action.

The kids all piled off the bus, gathering into a group to wait for further instructions, their non-stop chatter proof of the excitement.

Toby came to stand next to them. "Dad...when do we get to ride the horses? I can't wait to show Miss Sullivan what I've learned from my lessons. And Ava, of course," he added with a grin.

"Soon." Seth held up his hand to get the children's attention. "Listen up, kids. Mr. Devoe will be ready to start the rides in about ten minutes. He's got several horses and ranch hands to help keep things moving and you'll get a chance to ride a couple of times throughout the day, so don't worry. Relax and have fun, ask questions. Anything you want to know about the ranch, there are plenty of grownups to answer. Also, there's a BBQ lunch being set up, so whenever you get hungry, help yourself. And when you're not riding, there's the ball house, slide, horseshoes, and a soccer ball. Plenty to keep you busy. Above all...be safe."

"Yes, Mr. Dillinger," the kids all nodded, happily agreeing to get started. More like *get the horse on the trail.*

The kids all followed Susan toward the barn, eager to see the horses.

"I'm impressed, Mr. Dillinger. You seem to take the role of chaperone quite seriously," Leslie said, smiling up at him.

"Why, thank you. And if there's anything you need, don't be shy to ask. You and Susan should have as much fun as the kids, which is why we have several chaperone parents."

"*Hmmm*...I don't mind having fun. Not one bit. Someone went to a lot of trouble to put this together, so I reckon I can enjoy it." Leslie laughed, the sweet sound pleasing to his ears after missing it the past six weeks.

"Duty calls, so I need to get to work," Seth said, walking toward the group of kids all muddled about the horse paddock.

"Let's draw numbers for the order we ride." He pulled off his hat and dumped in the numbered papers he had put in his pocket this morning. They passed the hat around, each kid drawing a number and calling out the number. Ava, Toby's closest friend, was first up, her excitement genuine. The kids all lined up at the fence to watch, curious about what would happen. The last two tickets were for Leslie and Susan, and Seth let the older woman draw first.

"I've never actually ridden before. I had no idea you would include us in the riding plans for the day." Susan was giddy with excitement...like a school girl.

"Of course. Two special ladies taking excellent care of our kids and their education deserve the best," Seth said, happy to give back. These were dedicated teachers, and the entire community benefited from their efforts.

"Well, thank you. Truly," Susan said, her warm smile filled with appreciation.

He handed the last ticket to Leslie. "I've got to go help with the horses, but feel free to relax until it's your turn. And the food is ready to eat and comes highly recommended. Most of it came from the Golden Spoon, courtesy of Beverly Jenkins. As to the pork, it's been smoking all night and should be killer." Seth knew firsthand because he'd done the smoking...and the testing.

"For a chaperone, you sure are in take charge mode." Leslie laughed.

"That's because he *is* in charge. Seth put all this together," Susan said, letting his secret spill.

"You did?" Leslie asked, clearly shocked.

Seth shrugged. "Some of it. I had help."

"He was the mastermind event planner, and he even cooked the pork butt on the smoker. All night long."

"Seth? Are we talking about the same Seth?" Leslie teased.

"One and the same," Susan said.

"But who's tending the ranch?" Leslie asked, her brow lines deepening as she tried to understand. "I mean, you always said it was sunup to sundown, twenty-four seven," she added, a teasing light in her eyes.

"Dad's keeping an eye on things this morning. He's got strict instructions just to ride and check the pasture fences and keep an eye out for the new stallion being delivered today." That part had been a bit tricky because the final inspection for new livestock occurred at the time of delivery. With orders and deposits on the new foals, he and his father had agreed to parlay the money into a stallion and kick off the breeding center for other owners as a way to generate income during the long wait for the foals to arrive. Hopefully, it would allow them to add more mares to the ranch.

Seth had decided the time had come to trust his father's instincts more, knowing the man had grown up on the ranch and knew far more than he did. And in doing so, it allowed Seth to focus on what was more important.

Toby.

And winning Leslie's heart.

"Wow. I can't believe you cooked. Smoking BBQ is no easy task for a beginner. Are you sure its edible?" Leslie laughed.

"It is. Tested and approved...by more than just me," Seth added, secretly pleased with the camaraderie between them.

"You've come a long way in a short time. I'm so happy to hear everything is going well with you and your father. Family can be so important, even if we don't realize it right away."

"Thanks to you for steering me in the right direction. I'll have to think of a way to repay you." *Like dinner. For two.* But he wouldn't come right out and ask...not yet anyway.

"Just seeing the changes in Toby has been payment enough. He's like a whole new kid, excited to be at school. Making friends. He's more outgoing than I could have imagined. And he's a great helper to me and some of the other teachers." Leslie beamed, her gaze searching for Toby.

"That's what every parent wants to hear all about, but duty calls and I've got to run." Seth moved into the pen as the first mare was led out of the barn. "Thanks for doing this, Rusty."

"Anything for the kids. Of course, the free food offer didn't hurt." Rusty chuckled.

Two other men came out of the barn, leading a horse.

"We are going to run four mares at a time, first in the pen to get a feel for what each kid knows and a comfort level. From there, the guys will take any of the kids who are ready for the next level of a ride out on a one-on-one walk in the pasture and over to the creek, keeping a total focus on safety and the child. Any of the kids who aren't ready are free to have more rides in the pen to help them get more comfortable around horses. There will be several other ranch hands to assist at that point. We want to be fair to all and encourage a love of horses, not fear."

Toby had nothing but praise for his riding instructor, and Seth could see why. Rusty was a true professional that understood children and the different levels of readiness. A great quality to have when it came to the promotion of new activities and teaching children to trust. "Sounds like a great plan. I'll help wherever you need me to."

"Thanks. I planned on using you as one of the guides. Your knowledge and experience with horses comes in handy. Plus, I've seen you working with Toby and appreciate your level of patience."

High praise. "That works." And if Rusty had noticed, perhaps Leslie would too.

"Hey kids, I'm Rusty Devoe, the owner of the riding school. Mr. Dillinger has clued me in that you all want to ride horses. Is that right?" he asked, his voice loud enough to be heard above the excited conversations of the children.

"Yes, Mr. Devoe," most of the kids hollered, not to be outdone in their enthusiasm.

"Great. Then you've come to the right place. But first things first, please, call me Rusty. While I have your attention, we need to go over the rules to keep everyone safe and having a good time."

Rusty covered all the safety rules and talked about horses in general, making sure the kids knew enough of the basics to be lifted into the saddle for a ride. Seth stood back and watched but found his gaze drifting to Leslie. She was like a breath of fresh air and sunshine after weeks of not seeing her.

Leslie glanced his way and smiled. Seth's heart raced in response, his brain unable to maintain a slow speed as he tried to figure out what would happen next. Would she give him a chance or stay locked behind the rule wall she had erected between them?

One by one, the first four children were lifted onto the back of the horse. "What's your name?" Seth asked.

"Blake Andrews."

"It's nice to meet you, Blake. Have you ever ridden a horse before?" Seth asked, pushing aside all thoughts of Leslie as he focused on the child.

"No, sir. The horse is so much bigger from up here, and the ground is a long way away," Blake said, clutching the horn of the saddle.

"You are up off the ground quite a bit. But I also know your comment shows me you've got a keen sense of observation and a healthy touch of fear...which translates into respect. I think you'll do great riding. We'll take it nice and slow. Okay?"

The kid nodded, a shy smile on his face. "Okay."

Seth led the mare, following the ranch hand ahead of him. They made a slow walk around the ring, making sure to keep the horses evenly distanced.

"What do you think, Blake? Do you like riding?" Seth asked the boy as they drew to a stop ten minutes later.

"*Ummm*, I think so. Can I go again?" he asked.

"Of course, when it's your turn. Do you want me to tell Rusty you want to try a pasture ride?"

"Do you think I can do it?" Blake asked, looking unsure of himself.

"I do. But it's whether you believe in yourself that you can do it." A kid needed to have confidence in their ability, something Seth understood at a young age. Something his grandfather taught him.

"Then I do want to go in the pasture." Blake beamed.

"Then it's settled." Seth helped Blake dismount.

"That was so cool. Wait till I tell my mom. Toby is so lucky to have a cool dad like you."

"Thank you. And I'm pretty lucky to get to spend the day with all of you." It was something Seth vowed to do more often. He couldn't remember the last time he'd taken a day off to play. Although this might not fit the typical "play" heading, it was fun. Bringing joy to the children gave him a greater sense of peace and joy than he could have ever expected. It wasn't how many hours you put in the office or on the ranch. It was how much time you gave to your family and others around you. Their joy multiplied his own.

Seth looked up, and Leslie stood there expectantly. "What's up?"

"It's my turn to ride and you're the next guide," she teased, looking around the pen.

"So it is." He locked his hands together and helped her onto the horse. "First timer?" he asked, unwilling to assume anything.

Leslie shook her head. "No. I love horses, but it's been a while since I've ridden. Just never seem to have the time. I figured I'd go through the same paddock test as the children to show them we all need to follow the rules."

"Good thinking. You never told me you ride." But it was good to know there was something else they could share. A love of horses.

"There are a lot of things you don't know about me, Mr. Dillinger. But then when I was around, it was work, not play."

"Well then, we need to see what we can do to fix that." He handed her the reins and moved to the inside of the pen to watch. True to her words, she had no problem remembering how to ride. Which was a shame because it meant she wouldn't need a guide riding in the pasture. But there would be other times, at his ranch, he'd make sure of it in the future.

"Seth, can you give me a hand over here?" Rusty called out.

He waved, letting Rusty know he had heard. "Think you can handle finishing here?"

Leslie smiled. "Go ahead. I'll be fine." She seemed as though she wanted to say something, but clearly thought better of it as she clicked her heels on the horse's flanks and moved away.

Seth went to help Rusty, and before he knew it, hours had passed. Parenting a child was hard work, handling nineteen kids was a monster job and one that wore him out. As the afternoon drew to a close, the sound of country music coming from the barn reached his ears.

All afternoon, Leslie had stayed just as busy and Seth hadn't been able to put the other half of his plan into action. A slow song started, and he moved to stand beside her. "Will you dance with me?" Seth asked, holding out his hand. "Just two chaperones having fun," he said when she hesitated.

Leslie laid her hand in his and nodded. "Chaperones."

The slow country song was perfect for what Seth had in mind. He kept a space between them, so as not to set the town gossips running to the church, but enough there would be no doubt he was interested. The song ended, but Seth didn't release her hand.

Instead, he did a sweeping gesture with his hand and bowed to his lady love. The children laughed. He remembered one of the Shakespearean plays he'd been forced to watch in school but drew upon the memory now. "My lady, may I have another dance with you? A couple's dance for a couple," he added, laying his emotion on the line for all to see, and hoping she would say yes.

"I'm sorry…I don't date student's parents. You know the rules," she added softly, her eyes glassy as tears shimmered in their depths.

Seth knew she wanted to give him a different answer, and for him, that would be enough. *For now.* "Since changing schools isn't an option, I reckon we can be close friends until June." He winked. "You're worth waiting for." Seth leaned down to kiss her as a way to seal the deal. But it wasn't a dating kiss, more like a friendly kiss on the cheek. A lingering one, but still chaste.

But it was the squeeze of her hand that let him know she was all in.

Come summer, Seth vowed it would be a different kiss. But until then, he wanted his new best friend in his life knowing every day would bring new joys with her in it. *Starting tonight.*

"Will you come to dinner? As our guest?"

Leslie nodded. "I will, but I feel there's some things we need to discuss."

Seth was thrilled she had said yes, even if there was a qualifier. As though she were reluctant to agree.

False hope was the term that came to mind.

Chapter Twenty

♥

Leslie showered and headed for the Dillinger ranch, her nerves like fragile glass spikes waiting to break. She still couldn't believe Seth had asked her out, even after she'd warned him about school rules.

Granted, when she'd discussed it earlier, it was as a way to avoid him and help keep her focused in the right direction. The policy itself was a good one, but if two people truly cared for one another, they just needed to be patient. True love wouldn't slip away in the dark of the night when one wasn't looking.

Except now, he'd broken down the wall, or tried to, and it was confusing at best. The answer was no, as it was the only answer she should give at the moment. It was only when he pressed for "special friends," that Leslie knew she couldn't hide behind the school policy façade any longer. Seth was serious about moving them forward as a couple, something she desperately wanted, but wouldn't allow herself to dream about. Not while he didn't know her situation, and the real truth about why she avoided relationships.

It was something very personal and private, but there was no way she could have him hanging around until his son graduated to the second grade, only to find out the truth and people got hurt. Including Toby. Better to set Seth straight and deal with the fallout now.

Figuring out what to wear was just as difficult as what to say. She took out several outfits. Skirts. Jeans. A dress. And after about five combinations, gave up and grabbed the first one she'd tried on. The cream-colored cable-knit sweater was warm and comfortable. Not to mention a more relaxed look with jeans for an at home dinner.

The drive to the ranch only served to set her nerves more tightly wound. As she pulled up to the house, she couldn't help but notice the fresh coat of white paint, black shutters, and grand front porch lined with rockers. Toby had mentioned all the work being done at the ranch house, and of course, she'd heard about it from Claudia, but this was beyond her expectations. It reminded her of a luxury ranch home, the rolling pastures and white fences all divided up for as far as the eye could see.

No sooner had she arrived, than Seth met her on the porch. Taking her by the hand, he led her inside the house. "Look who's here, Toby."

"Miss Sullivan, you came. Did you bring Jelly?" Toby asked, a hopeful expression on his face.

Leslie smiled, hugging Toby's shoulder lightly. "Not this time. I would need to clear it with your dad first. Thanks for asking me to dinner."

"My father had to leave for Austin, so there's plenty of food and there will be plenty of leftovers. I just hope you approve of my cooking, seeing as I'm only just learning. Betty Crocker has a good book," Seth teased.

"I'm sure it will be just fine. I have it on good authority you can read and smoke a pork butt," Leslie said, grinning. "The house looks gorgeous. I can't believe how much you got done." The front living room had beautiful gold drapes that accented the hardwood floors and oversized picture windows. The early evening sky had turned pink, casting a glow over the room.

"Thanks. I had a lot of help, but knew getting it finished was important to us and our ability to get settled in. A sense of belonging."

"Well, I'd say you succeeded quite nicely. And I know Toby's been doing great at school as well. It all goes hand in hand," Leslie said.

"I see that now, thanks to you. Dinner's ready if you are."

"Sounds good to me," Leslie said, following Toby into the dining room. She admired the new wagon-wheel chandelier with its five lantern globes. Everything in the house, it would seem had been coordinated with a modern rustic touch, and it worked beautifully.

"I want to ask the blessing," Toby said as they all sat down.

"How sweet," Leslie said, closing her eyes and bowing her head.

"God is great. God is good. Let us thank him for our food. Amen."

"Nice work, son." Seth smiled at Toby and nodded.

It was a simple, but long-standing prayer children learned early on. And it was always a good fallback for adults who got nervous praying out loud. She should know. Talking in front of people always made her uncomfortable. Adult people, that is. Kids...they were different. They always paid attention and made her feel special.

"*Hmmm.* This stew is good. You need not have worried. Did you use—"

"The leftovers from today." Seth grinned. "Yes. I thought it would add a nice smoky flavor," he said, obviously pleased the stew had turned out good.

"I helped," Toby beamed, not one to be left out.

"Thank you. I'm glad it passes muster," Seth said, passing her the basket of bread. "Store bought, of course. I wasn't about to try my hand at something so complex."

"This will be perfect. Especially if you pass me the butter. Butter makes everything delicious," Leslie said, grinning at him.

"My grandparents thought the same thing." Seth chuckled.

The rest of the dinner was full of non-stop conversation, Toby leading the way. And after everything was cleaned up, they settled in to play a few games. Time flew past, everyone winning at least once, which kept Toby happy.

Seth glanced at his watch. "Time for bed, young man."

"Do I have to?" Toby asked, yawning at the same time.

"Absolutely."

"Aww, shucks. Goodnight Miss Sullivan."

"Good night, Toby."

"Wait right here, and I'll be back in a second," Seth said, following Toby out of the room.

Leslie folded the afghan on the sofa, her nerves returning to their former state of unrest. She moved about the room, looking at pictures on the wall, and taking full stock of the changes. Seth and his father had done a beautiful job remodeling the place. It was fresh and warm. *Homey*. It was the kind of house she one day dreamed of having with a large kitchen and attached great room. The picture was complete with a roaring fire in the stone fireplace.

"Toby's exhausted after today, but I think he would have tried to stay up all night knowing you're here," Seth said, coming into the room.

"He's such a sweetheart," she said. It was the greatest compliment a child could pay an adult...wanting to spend time with them.

"Would you like a glass of tea or lemonade?" Seth asked.

"No thanks. I had plenty at dinner." Not to mention, if she held a glass in her hands, Seth would be left without a doubt as to the state of her nerves.

"Okay, then. You said you wanted to talk, so let's talk," he said, taking her by the hand and leading her to the two chairs closest to the fireplace.

Cozy. Other than the anxiety that left her heart pounding. The time had come to tell Seth the truth and there was no putting it off any further. It would be easier if they were dating, talking about these sorts of things. But they weren't dating.

Special friends.

Friends shared most everything. If she put it into context, it would be like confiding in Beth. "This is a little awkward, but I'm going to have to come right out and tell you some things about me, given your earlier declaration."

"Go on, I'm listening." Seth leaned back in his seat.

"First, let me say, I'm not averse to moving forward, as you mentioned, but it would come at a price. One, I feel you need to know before we go any further." Leslie twisted her hands together in her lap, trying to quell the anxiety.

"Nothing you have to say will change what I want with you. A relationship, that is. Unless you're married. That would be a deal breaker." Seth laughed, but suddenly stopped. "You're not, right?"

Leslie stared into the fire, unable to face Seth. "Not married. But...I can't have children." There... she had said the dreaded words, choking back the pain they always caused.

"I see. Is this a medical condition then?" he asked.

There wasn't a hint of distaste in the question or his tone. Leslie steeled herself to face him. "It is. I had endometriosis when I was younger and it left me unable to have children. My doctor said I would most likely never conceive, based on the severity of the damage from the disease and scarred fallopian tubes." She brushed away the tears that rolled down her cheeks, despite all efforts to hold them back.

Seth moved to kneel at her feet, taking her hands in his. "Well, then it's a good thing we have Toby. You do realize we haven't even dated and we're talking about having children. It's a bit unorthodox," he teased, a gentle smile tugging at his lips.

Perhaps he didn't understand all that her condition would mean. It was easy to dismiss it now, but what if they got married? The next natural course would be children. And yes, they had Toby, but what if Seth wanted more kids And what of her...she knew what she wanted. "True. But I don't want to do this "special friend" thing, fall in love with you, and then have my condition be an issue. A deal breaker that leads to a heartbreaker. No thanks."

"I'm not trying to make light of your medical condition. Trust me. And you have a good point, but as I said, there's Toby. And if you want more children, there's always adoption.

So not a deal breaker for me." Seth pressed a kiss to the back of her hand.

She believed him. Beth had been right all along. Any man that truly cared for her would find a way to make things work. *Unlike Brad.* He simply wasn't the right guy. Not even close. "Thank you. I've thought about adopting, but I'm not quite ready and I know they frown on single parenting. But it's nice to know you would consider that as a possibility...given that come June we want to date, that is." The humor of the situation struck Leslie full force, and she burst out laughing, unable to come to grips with all that had transpired in the last few minutes.

Seth pulled her to her feet. "Oh, I'll want to date, alright. I figure this gives us a chance to work on being friends first. You know, be on the same team. Time to grow...together. It was something lacking in my first marriage."

"I see. Well then, perhaps we can make this work after all. Thank you for understanding. In the end, it's best for Toby. The policy is there to protect the children. As for me, it was easier to hide behind the school rules than to face my shortcomings and fears when it came to relationships."

"Believe it or not, I understand and appreciate what the school is trying to do. I've learned to be a patient man, Leslie, and I figure you're worth waiting for."

Leslie blushed. "I really need to get going now that we have this settled. Jelly still needs to go out for a potty break, and I've got to meet Beth for breakfast." The truth was, with everything out in the open, she felt a little awkward. How did one be friends with the man she wanted to kiss?

"I'll walk you to the car," Seth said, picking up her sweater.

"That won't be necessary. We're just friends and I can walk myself." Leslie smiled up at him, resisting the urge to make a move. This time it would be her sending the wrong message.

"And friends take care of friends. Humor me," Seth said, leading her outside. They stood by the car, the full moon shining down brightly.

"How beautiful it is out here, the moonlight flooding the countryside with a warm glow," Leslie said, taking in the magnificence of the evening and the man standing next to her.

"Yes, it's almost as beautiful as you are," Seth said, taking her hand and pulling her close.

Leslie knew she should move away. It complicated things, and it wasn't allowed. But it was no more than she wanted. She just didn't have the nerve to see it through on her own. "Seth," she said, her voice breathless.

Seth cupped her chin with one hand and lowered his head, his mouth stopping mere inches from hers. "It's just one kiss to last us till summer. Until all this is over and I can kiss you anytime I want."

He moved closer, his lips claiming her in a sweet kiss. There was no Toby to interrupt and Leslie had no intention of stopping him.

All too soon, it was over, the cool evening air replacing his mouth. "In that case, perhaps you should make it two. Just to make sure we remember." Leslie lifted her face and moved in close.

"Anything you wish," Seth said, lowering his mouth to hers once again.

Leslie wanted to etch this moment in her brain for all eternity.

Luckily, the school year would come to an end...just like it did every year. Only this time there would be a sweet and handsome cowboy waiting for her.

Epilogue

June rolled around, marking the end of first grade for Toby. From there, summer had been a whirlwind of events.

The official first day of summer vacation marked the first day Seth had taken Leslie on a dinner date for two...a romantic, candlelit dinner. One that ended with a kiss and was the beginning for her and Seth as a couple.

By July, they were officially engaged, much to the delight of Toby and everyone in town. It's not like people didn't know they cared about each other, but they stuck with the plan.

By early August, they were married. A barn wedding, and one most of the community attended. After all, Leslie had taught most of their children...either in elementary school or in Sunday school.

Before Leslie knew it, Fall rolled in and life in her new home and with her new family had all fallen into place, not without issue, but then so much had happened so quickly. It was to be expected.

She stepped out onto the porch and pulled her jacket tighter. A cold, brisk wind blew in cooler temperatures with Thanksgiving just around the corner. The house was decorated, with every room festive and bright. She had a family, and that was more than enough to be thankful for.

For the past couple of months she'd felt run down and tired but stood firm in her belief it was just all the changes and settling in at the ranch, all while managing both her jobs and taking on the role of mother and wife. Two titles she repeated over and over to herself, hardly believing they were true.

Jelly barked in the distance, as she ran with Toby around the yard, Claudia not far away and watching them. It had taken some doing, but Seth had finally convinced Leslie to see a doctor, and Claudia had agreed to come over and keep an eye on Toby.

"Ready to go?" Seth asked, stepping out onto the porch behind Leslie.

"Sure thing. If it will get you to stop pestering me." She laughed, truly not upset that someone cared this much about her wellbeing. Love had a way of wrapping itself around you and holding tight.

"As long as you don't ask me to stop loving you, then I guess I can live with anything." Seth dropped a kiss on her mouth before leading her to the car.

"Were the foals okay?" Leslie asked. They were the most adorable Dutch Warmblood fillies and they stayed closed to their mothers. It touched her heart to see the bond forming and their playful silliness as they raced around the pasture. She hadn't said anything to Seth, but the idea of them going to new homes was upsetting.

"They're doing great. Tom and Bill came by to have a look and this time, Tom brought his son. It reminded me of Toby's reaction when the mares foaled. The vet will be here tomorrow for a checkup. Oh, and I forgot to tell you, we have two more breeders coming out next week. Business is picking up."

"I always did believe in you."

"I believed in us." Seth smiled and took her hand, leading her into the doctor's office. Ten minutes later, they were checked in and ushered into one of the patient rooms. The nurse drew some blood. Preliminary testing is what she called it. Almost thirty minutes later, Dr. Miller joined them. It was time for answers.

"Sorry for the delay, but we got backed up a little this morning. But it's all good because I reckon we can cut this visit short." He grinned. "There's nothing wrong with you Leslie that a little rest won't fix."

"See, I told you Seth. My husband has been so worried. It's just a bug or something, right?" Leslie asked, relieved to hear the doctor's assessment. Secretly, she too had been concerned, but hadn't let on to Seth or she never would have heard the end of it.

"Or something. About the only thing similar is that it starts with a B. As in baby." The doctor dropped the bomb, taking them by surprise.

Leslie couldn't possibly have heard Dr. Miller right. She looked at Seth, satisfied to see he was just as confused and speechless. Turning back to the doctor, she cleared her head and tried to focus. "Baby...as in I'm having a baby?" she asked, desperately wanting the news to be true.

The doctor nodded. "Absolutely."

"But how?" she asked, her brain still numb from the news. Elated...but numb.

"The same way babies are generally conceived, I reckon," Dr. Miller teased.

"But you said—"

"I know, but clearly, I was wrong. It happens, but not often. And it's not unusual for a woman who had endometriosis when they do get pregnant, to continue having periods for a few months. That's what makes it hard to figure out at first."

Pregnant. They were having a baby. *Nothing was impossible for God.*

Seth reached for her hand and pulled her into his arms. "A baby," he said, grinning down at her. "Just when I thought life couldn't get any better."

"Looks like you were right to get me to the doctor's office after all, Mr. Dillinger," she teased.

"Keep that in mind for next time, Mrs. Dillinger." Seth kissed her, not at all caring about the doctor looking on. It was probably one of the highlights of the man's job, delivering good news.

"How far along do you think I am?" Leslie asked.

"I would say three months, give or take a week. You two work fast." The doctor chuckled. "It also means you're safely out of the first trimester and that we should be able to find out if it's a boy or girl next month, if you want to know that is."

"Or we could be surprised. Whatever Leslie wants is fine by me," Seth offered. His consideration for others knew no bounds, and it was one of the things she loved about him.

"It's probably easier to know so that we can get the room ready. I want it to be perfect," Leslie said, coming to a decision. There would be so much to get done, and she wanted to enjoy the whole journey.

Seth dropped a kiss on her forehead. "Everything will be because the baby has you as a mother."

The doctor slipped out of the room, leaving the two of them alone.

"And you as a father. Let's go tell Toby. I can't wait to tell him," Leslie said, taking Seth by the hand as they left the doctor's office. A new future they would share together.

Good news did come in small packages.

Thank you, Lord.

Six months later...

Seth couldn't have been any happier as he held Baby Kendra Dillinger in his arms for the first time. The baby had made her entrance into the world at eleven-fifty-eight p.m. The same day Seth and Leslie officially started dating and admitted their love for each other. It was a day that would always be special, but now, for more reasons than they could have foreseen. And with Toby as a big brother, Kendra would have more than enough love as she grew older.

But for now, Seth wanted to focus on the present and enjoy every minute that life had to offer. Once he set his priorities straight, life had fallen right into line.

The horse ranch was doing well, the place a tribute to his grandparents. Grandpa Dillinger was doing well and took great pleasure in his grandson and would cherish his granddaughter equally.

And as for Toby, he now owned Peanut Butter, a dog of his very own.

Seth's return to Crossroads Creek had turned his life around...*all for the best and for the glory of God, he'd found his true love and happiness.*

If you enjoyed this sweet and charming romance, be sure to check out the
ALSO BY ELSIE DAVIS section on the next page for more clean and wholesome romance.

BONUS READ

Want to keep in touch with new releases and what's happening in the world of Elsie Davis? Sign up for the monthly newsletter at Elsie Davis HEA (Happily-Ever-After) and enjoy DIGGING THE DRIVER (A Celebrity Corgi Romance) as a FREE BOOK!

The greatest compliment you could give an author is to leave a review in order to help other readers discover the same great stories you enjoyed. Amazon/Bookbub/Goodreads are all great places. Many thanks!!!

Another great way to keep in touch - *Follow Elsie Davis on FaceBook*

Also By Elsie Davis

Sweet, Clean and Wholesome Stories...with a Happily-Ever-After Guarantee!

Holidays in Hallbrook
(Sweet Romance Series for Holidays Throughout the Year)
Welcome to Hallbrook, New Hampshire. A small-town filled with the unexpected, lots of love, and of course, a beloved dog to ramp up the excitement.
Love & Order (Labor Day)
Love & Family (Thanksgiving)
Love & Peace (Christmas)
Love & Chocolate (Valentine's Day)
Love & Hope (Mother's Day)
Love & Liberty (Independence Day)

Love & Honor (Veteran's Day)
Love & Joy (Easter)
Love & Adventure (Father's Day)

Great Smoky Mountain Getaways
(Christian Inspirational – Women's Fiction Romances)
Juliet's Journey to Love
Poppy's Path to Love
Rachel's Road to Love

Crossroads Creek Cowboys
(Christian Inspirational Romances)
The Heart of a Cowboy
The Help of a Cowboy
The Return of a Cowboy
Coming Soon – The Care of a Cowboy

Crestfield Inn Romances

If you like special kinds of soulmates, a splash of the supernatural, and wholesome relationships, you'll adore this sweet bit of fun filled with romance and mystery.
Turning Back Time
Turning Up Roses
Turning Down Pie

Celebrity Corgi Romance
(Standalone Sweet Romance)
If you like light mystery mixed in with your happily-ever-after, you'll enjoy this second-chance romance and the race to save an adorable Corgi.
Digging the Driver

Gold Coast Retrievers
(Sweet Romance)
Special Golden Retrievers help their humans solve mysteries, save lives, and even find love...

Defending Dakota

Trinity River
(Sweet Western Romance)
Ranchers and farmers depend on the Trinity River for water, but when a secret conglomerate starts buying up property by fair means or foul, it's time for the landowners of Tumble County to fight back—Texas style. But what they don't count on, is finding love in the process.
Back in the Rancher's Arms
Small Town, Big Secrets

Coming Soon! (2023-2024)

Sundancer's Legacy – 9 Book series

Sundancer's Star
Sundancer's Joy
Sundancer's Heart

Sundancer's Majesty
Sundancer's Miracle
Sundancer's Glory
Sundancer's Kiss
Sundancer's Moon
Sundancer's Splendor

About The Author

Elsie Davis is a *USA Today and International Bestselling Author* of over 25 sweet, clean, and wholesome romances, and a member of the ACFW. She discovered the world of Happily-Ever-After romance at the age of twelve when she began avidly reading Barbara Cartland, the Queen of Romance, and has been hooked ever since. After building her dream log home on top of a small mountain, she turned her attention to do what she loves most, writing. Elsie writes sweet Contemporary Romance and Contemporary Christian Romance from her heart...hoping to share a little love in a big world.

When she's not writing, she can be found birding, kayaking, camping, fishing, playing disc golf, and taking nature walks—hoping to

spot wildlife. Basically, she loves all things outdoors, EXCEPT cold weather. She and her husband are avid Caribbean cruisers, but Elsie's
favorite vacation was their cruise to Alaska. (In
spite of the cold!) Indoors, she enjoys a toasty
fire, and of course, a great romance with a guar-
anteed Happily-Ever-After.

<u>https://www.elsiedavishea.com</u>